BRANDED

THAT OLD BLACK MAGIC, HEART'S DESIRED MATE SERIES

ANN GIMPEL

CONTENTS

BRANDED

THAT OLD BLACK MAGIC ROMANCE

Heart's Desired Mate Series
Paranormal Romance
By
Ann Gimpel

Copyright Page

Nothing ever happens in sleepy little Stillwater, California, which was exactly why Liam settled there. What better spot to avoid discovery? Banished by his dragon-shifter kinsmen for sexual improprieties, his sentence has ten years to go. The only snag is he has to find a mate before he can return to Xara, the dragons' home world.

Aisha has a problem. She's stuck tending a herd of Arabians, and she'll be there forever if she doesn't produce another witch to take over. To do that, she needs a man. No one permanent. Just someone to grace her bed long enough to get her pregnant.

Intent on fulfilling her obligation to the Colewright witches, Aisha casts a love charm aimed right at Liam. She has no idea what he is—or that his magic overshadows hers by a country mile—and her spell backfires. Badly. She's picking up the pieces, determined to move past the humiliation, but Liam has other ideas. Lots of them.

CHAPTER 1

"Hey, dude, slow down." Hal's words were thin, strained. He was trying to sound cool, but tension bled through.

"I can't stop right here. Relax. I won't let you fall. You're roped in," Liam Fiontan called back. The music of Scotland still ran through his speech, and he missed hearing it in the flat, nasal twang of Americanized English.

"You'll run out of rope."

Heat began in Liam's belly. Before things got totally out of hand and a gout of fire blasted through his mouth—tough to explain something like that away—he focused on the granite beneath his fingertips. Smooth, but with nubs in all the right places, it was his favorite kind of climbing.

He could have free-climbed this pitch, but he wasn't deep in the mountains for himself today. Nope. Today, he was guiding another human klutz. In exactly ten years, thirty-five days, and ten minutes, his enforced exile in this godawful place would be done. Then he'd return to Xara, where he could take to his dragon form whenever he wanted. The way he felt right this minute, he didn't care if he was ever human again.

"Good to finally be appreciated," his dragon commented dryly, and a small thread of smoke trailed from Liam's nostrils. He hoped to hell Hal was too spun out to notice.

Ten years, thirty-five days, and ten minutes, and he could go home. No one would have the right to bar the doors of the world he'd been born into thousands of years before.

Unless he showed up without a mate. The way things were going, that might turn into the deal breaker that kept him earthbound.

When the world was younger, and Atlantis fell into the North Sea, Xara took its place. Shielded from Earth by a series of enchanted veils, a particular series of notes was required to open them. Anything different, and the would-be sojourner lost his life.

It kept the riffraff out. Except the musical code had been altered to exclude him too. He gnashed his teeth. His enforced exile still pissed the holy crap out of him.

"Why haven't you stopped? Is something wrong?" Hal called, the frantic note back in his voice. "Pay attention! We're down to maybe twenty-five feet of rope."

Liam squelched a desire to draw the knife from where it hung in a sheath off his hardware belt and cut the goddamned rope. See how much Hal liked it then.

Patience. Compassion.

He repeated the two words like a mantra and searched for a spot he could tie off and belay his client up the dicey part of this multipitch climb. Hal didn't have much experience, which was why he'd hired Liam.

"See that knob?" Liam pointed. Without waiting for Hal to reply, he went on, "There's a tiny ledge and a place for me set up a belay. Five more minutes."

"The rope," Hal persisted.

"There'll be plenty left. You'll see."

Liam scrambled upward, trying for credible moves as he felt Hal's gaze glued to him. Now wasn't the time for gravity-defying stunts. The mood Hal was in, anything that felt weird might send him spinning over a metaphorical edge.

Reaching the rock protuberance, Liam looped the rope around it.

"Okay. Come on up."

"It's about fucking time," Hal mumbled, probably assuming Liam couldn't hear him. Had he been human, that assumption would have held water, but dragons had very keen ears.

As he waited for Hal to haul his out-of-shape body upward, scrabbling for easy holds and then losing them, Liam yearned for his winged form, replete with coppery-green scales. He shifted, but only on nights with no moon, and he never flew very far. With modern technology, all it would take would be one over-zealous jackass with a high-powered rifle fitted with a night scope to notice him. They could shoot all they wanted. Bullets wouldn't penetrate his hide, and even if they did, he was damned close to immortal. The damage to being spotted would come from live footage on social media that would turn viral overnight.

He winced at likely headlines blasting over every platform. Maybe they wouldn't call him a dragon, because men today didn't believe such things existed. Whatever they labeled him instead would probably annoy him so much, he'd go off the deep end and chase down the idiot who'd began the whole mess, leaving broken heads and bones in the wake of his wrath.

And blood. Plenty of bright, red blood.

Just thinking about it made his heart thud hard and his nostrils flare with anticipation. Life today was far too sanitized. Men needed bloody, to-the-death fights to be, well, men. The current batch was nothing but a bunch of pussies.

Ninety years down. Ten to go. He forced a steadying breath, followed by one more. At least his vision, which had taken on the layered aspect it held as a dragon, returned to its human attributes.

He'd settled in the backwater town of Stillwater, California about fifteen years ago. He didn't think he could remain ten more years without people noticing he hadn't aged at all, which meant he'd have to pull up stakes—again.

He glanced down, checking on Hal. "Doing great there, buddy," he yelled.

Hal turned a sweat-streaked face upward. His blue eyes were bloodshot, and strands of dark hair were plastered to his forehead. "I don't see how you make it look so easy."

Because I'm not human...

"Years of practice, mate. You can stop and breathe a bit. No rush. Plenty of daylight left."

Liam checked the rope out of habit. It hadn't moved, but he hadn't expected it to. He was good at what he did. He'd had a pile of crappy jobs over the span of years since he'd been booted from Xara for the crime of using magic to seduce Kai, his cousin's mate.

Farrier. Mechanic. Bartender.

Starting his own mountain guide service had been little shy of brilliant. It allowed him to be outside, oftentimes alone as he scouted routes, and it afforded more shifting opportunities than he'd had since leaving Xara.

Beyond that, his clients paid well and tipped him on top of his fees.

Not that the dragon tribunal hadn't been within their rights exiling him. He'd gone a wee bit overboard with his seduction scheme. Kai had actually believed she was having sex with her mate, Grigori. She'd been livid—and gorgeous—when she'd discovered the truth, fire spewing from her mouth in huge splats of fury that made him hard all over again just thinking about it.

Liam clenched his jaw hard enough to make the bones hurt. His other task while on Earth was to locate a mate of his own. He might have ten years left, but aside from bedding a series of lissome maids, he hadn't found anyone he wanted to spend eternity with. Dragon shifters didn't recognize divorce. Matings were final, which made the selection process so important.

Not only had he not managed to locate a potential mate, he'd quit trying half a century before. When he'd broached the topic of other worlds and other cultures—on a purely philosophical basis, of course—he'd been met with jeers or suggestions he'd had a few too many shots of whiskey. Even if he'd fallen in love, it was doubtful the lass would be so smitten she'd have agreed to leaving home and hearth to undergo the ritual that would turn her into a dragon shifter like him.

No choice there. Only dragon shifters were allowed past Xara's boundaries. He needed a mate to return, ergo the mate had to be a dragon shifter. Case closed.

Hardware rattled, alerting him his client was close. He gripped Hal's harness, dragging him the last foot onto his belay ledge. Liam wrinkled his nose but stopped shy of telling his client he stank. Fear sweat was the worst, and it hung around Hal in a thick, cloying miasma reminiscent of salty, overripe trash.

"Jesus, that was hard." Breath steamed from Hal, and he swiped his forearm across his wet forehead.

"The rest is easier, and then we have a choice." Liam infused a confident calm into his words, more for himself than his client. Hal was far more inept than most of his customers.

"What kind of choice?" Suspicion beat a tattoo beneath Hal's question.

Liam turned to face him squarely, a neat trick on the four-inch ledge. "You'd have an easier time if you trusted me, mate. I have an impeccable track record. I've never lost a client. You won't be the first."

Hal's cheeks, already red, grew more colorful, and he looked away. "Sorry. I know I'm not very brave. It's why I want to learn how to do shit like this."

"You're doing okay." Liam forced a crooked smile. "You could have bailed five feet off the ground, but you're still here."

Hal grinned back. "Yeah, I guess I am. Lead on."

"Nope. Your turn to lead. This next part is easy. Class three-four."

Hal's grin widened. "Are you sure?"

"You bet, I'm sure." Liam scooted over to make room for Hal to climb past him.

IT WAS full dark by the time they reached the trailhead where Liam tucked Hal into his car and watched him drive away. Pushing Hal into leading the last two hundred feet of easy climbing had done worlds for the man's self-confidence. He'd thanked Liam profusely, and tipped generously.

Liam snorted, and a few flames shot from his nose. Paper money lacked the panache of gold and gemstones, but what the hell. No one used gold anymore. It was mostly relegated to collectors and museums. The glow from the car's taillights vanished in the murk, and he tossed hardware into the back of his ancient Chevy 4-wheel-drive pickup. It had been green originally but had turned to a mélange of rust and faded patina.

He unbuckled his pack and tossed it atop the hardware, breathing in fresh, mountain air, redolent with the scents of pine and small, nesting rodents. They were all in their dens this time of year, living off food stocks they'd laid in during the summer months. Having Hal ahead of him had offered hours of thinking time.

For once, Liam took advantage of it. Usually, he blanked his mind, but he needed a plan. Stillwater was an odd place. Other magical beings lived there, but they played their paranormal ability very close to the vest. He hadn't wanted to rock anyone's illusion they were passing as human, so he kept to himself. Besides, what would he say?

"Hey, there, lass! You're looking a whole lot like a witch to me."

Or, "Bollocks, mate. Are you a shifter too?"

Not that Stillwater held any other dragon shifters —none that he knew of anyway. Just an assortment of wolves, bears, coyotes, and birds.

Of course, there wouldn't be dragon shifters. They all lived in Xara just like he used to.

He screwed his face into a grimace. The other problem with outing anyone magical was it would reveal he couldn't be human, either. Saying anything was fraught with glitches, and he far preferred to keep his life as simple as possible.

It wasn't hard. He lived a few miles outside town at the very end of a rocky, rutted dirt road where he barely had Internet or cellular service. He enjoyed the privacy, but he also maintained a small office in town. It was where he met clients. Last thing he wanted was for his clients—or anyone else—to know where he lived. If an errant soul decided to drop in on him while he was either between forms, or fully dragonesque, it would be impossible to explain. He could use magic to wipe someone's memories, but he wasn't certain how well it would work on another magic wielder.

He'd wound wards around his grotto not to protect the rustic log cabin but to ensure no one found the entrance to his cave. Another snort rumbled past his lips, followed by steam. The cave was actually a mine, and the cabin had once belonged to whoever worked it, but the tapped-out gold mine made a perfect spot to conceal his hoard, an opportunity that had eluded him before moving to Stillwater.

He'd amassed small stashes before, but they'd been stolen—twice.

The first time, he'd killed the miscreant who'd pilfered his gold and gems, and nearly been caught. That little incident happened during the early years of his exile, before the advent of state-of-the-art police aids like DNA testing. He'd taken care to be far more circumspect after that.

And ridden herd on his temper.

The dragons' covenant gave him an absolute right to kill anyone—human or otherwise—pilfering from his hoard, but he doubted those laws would hold up here on Earth. Merely mentioning them would like as not be enough to get him sent off for a mental evaluation.

In truth, the abandoned mine was one reason he'd remained in Stillwater as long as he had. He loved wandering into its deep shafts and letting the small hoard he'd collected run through his fingers. He'd even shifted within the mine and lain atop his treasure, loving the feel of it beneath his belly.

He sent power zinging outward. He hadn't heard a car since Hal left, but people could be camped in the nearby wilderness. It might be dark, but a half moon had just crested the horizon. He wanted to shift. This was a perfect spot, but not if he ran the risk of discovery.

His nostrils flared as he scented the air, savoring his solitude. Between cell phones and the Internet, no one was truly alone anymore. Ever. Maybe that was what was wrong with people. They never figured out who they were since their signals were forever bouncing off everyone else in an infinite tape loop spouting gibberish.

Kind of like a digitized Tower of Babel.

The analogy made him grin.

He tucked the keys beneath a tire and stripped out of his clothes, folding them neatly and stashing them behind a nearby boulder. He had second thoughts about the keys, retrieved them, and left them with his clothing, tossing an obfuscation spell over the whole mess.

Spreading his arms, he let the shift magic take him. As soon as he had wings, he pumped them hard and rose into the night amid the clean, righteous sound of his scales clanking against one another. For the next few glorious moments, he didn't think about anything beyond the wonder of flight as his wings cleaved air thicker than Xara's atmosphere. He had to work harder to gain altitude, but once there, the sturdier air made it easier to remain airborne.

A flicker of movement caught his keen eyes. A small herd of elk had stopped beneath an evergreen canopy to drink at a fast-moving mountain stream. Fools! They weren't even bothering to scan the skies, but why should they? In their world, hunters were tethered to the land, just like they were.

Once he realized he was flirting with a stealth attack, he reined himself in. If he killed the fat buck he had his eye on, he'd be stuck eating it where it fell. Flying it back to his truck was risky. Even chancier would be driving home with poached prey. It wasn't hunting season, and even if it were, he didn't have a license.

Pfft. Men were stupid and narrow-minded. No one should need a license to kill anything. He almost choked on more fire that wanted out. He'd paint the skies with his outrage—if he were anywhere but here.

The joy that had filled him frittered to dregs. This wasn't Xara. He couldn't hunt for whatever drew him. Why the hell hadn't he gotten used to the status quo? He'd been here plenty long enough to move beyond falling into a funk when truth slapped him in the face.

A flash of headlights brought reality crashing down fast. He wasn't alone anymore. And it wasn't very dark. If the occupants of the SUV cruising along mountain roads twisting below him were a posse of illegal hunters, they'd use high-powered lights. Not that they'd be focused on the skies, but what if one of them looked up?

He curled his taloned forefeet into hard knots of anger. Fire shot from his mouth before he got the primal parts of himself under ragged control. These were his mountains. *His.* The interlopers had no rights. He could blast their puny automobile, turn it into a heap of smoking, twisted metal.

Yeah. And the minute I do something like that, I'll have to leave Stillwater. Remaining would be too big a gamble.

Leaving Stillwater meant leaving his cave, and he wasn't ready to give it up. Not yet.

He wasn't able to shroud his dragon body with invisibility spells. As a fallback measure, he cast a don't-look-here enchantment and flew in a straight line back to his truck. He left the SUV that had no business in his territory behind without incident and shifted in a blaze of light before his feet contacted the ground.

Not much he could do about the last part. Shifting without fanfare wasn't possible. He dressed fast, trying to latch onto the simple pleasure that had rolled through him while he was airborne. It eluded him. All that remained was hollow resignation.

If he couldn't locate a mate, he couldn't return to Xara. It was part of his punishment, the part designed to ensure he'd never trick another mated dragon shifter into sharing his bed. Not only were dragon pairings permanent, the partners were always faithful to one another. Even the ones who'd stopped having sex never took another lover.

He slid his jacket on over his top and raked his hands through his shoulder-length hair. Settling in with a mate meant the end of fun. The end of experimentation. The end of spying a lovely, buxom lassie and plotting to bed her.

"Oh for fuck's sake," he muttered. "How many times have I done that lately? Zero. Minus zero if you consider how long it's been since my cock's seen aught but my hand."

He splayed his fingers over the chilly metal hood of the Chevy, half expecting talons to form.

They didn't.

At least he was facing his problems tonight, not circumventing them like he usually did. What it came down to was simple enough. Did he want his freedom more than Xara? Or did returning home trump everything?

Forever was a long time to remain alone. A long time to be an exile, repudiating his true nature. A long time to string one-night stands together—if he ever found the energy to sink into seductions again.

He pressed his fingers into the metal, not surprised when it dented beneath his touch. Nothing in this godforsaken place was built to last, but why should it be? Men didn't live very long. Never mind products rolling out of their factories didn't even match their puny lifespans.

He pushed harder, deepening the dents. He was missing the point. This wasn't about shoddy quality. It was about him and what he wanted. He had to make a choice and stick with it. No more games. No more jokes. No more putting everything off for another day.

He pulled the car door open, amid the protest of rusty hinges and aging metal, and jumped nimbly into the driver's seat. For once, the high-mileage engine kicked over the first time he tapped the ignition. Maybe it sensed his foul mood.

He nosed the truck around and started toward home, forcing an open mind, one where thoughts bubbled up as they formed. He wasn't even off the mountain before disgust for the half-life he'd been living coated his tongue with a bitter residue.

Hiding his dragon nature went against the grain. He may not agree with his kinfolks about mating—or anything else—but he'd suck up his misgivings. He needed to return to Xara. Needed to offer his dragon far more than the occasional furtive flight and pathetic hoard.

A sense of peace flowed from his midsection outward as he nudged the truck through a dark and silent Stillwater and thence toward his purloined miner's shack. Inner harmony, where he wasn't fighting himself, had dodged him since his exile. He welcomed the strength that came from not engaging in constant Socratic dialogue. Or anger. While a great diversion, it never solved anything.

"I made a decision," he muttered to the darkened

cab. "It feels right, but where the hell will I find a mate?"

He ground his teeth in frustration. Probably not in Stillwater, but he'd been thinking about leaving, anyway. Maybe sooner rather than later would be just the ticket.

CHAPTER 2

Aisha Colewright built her nightly spell around the stable housing a dozen Arabians. The horses whickered in response to the feel of her magic bathing them with protection. She raised them and sold them, just like her mother and grandmother had done before her. Many of her customers came from other countries, but she always insisted they show up at her ranch before she agreed to let them purchase any of her stock. Nothing like meeting someone up close and personal to assess if they'd provide an acceptable home for her darlings.

Satisfied nothing would disturb her babies through the night, she started across the expanse of yard between the barn and the house. The evening was cold and clear, the sky shot with millions of stars. She wrapped her arms around herself and stopped, gazing at the wonder scattered above. She'd always wanted to fly, but contrary to urban myths about witches and their broomsticks, flight wasn't part of any witch's supernatural bag of tricks.

A crackle of magic jigged across the blackness, and she cocked her head to one side wondering what spawned it. Stillwater was home to a hodgepodge of magical types, but most of them didn't hold all that much power. Plus, it wasn't the kind of thing that ever entered polite conversation. Humans still held a clear majority in her small town—everywhere else as well— and an unspoken code among those like her was to downplay any and all paranormal abilities.

She curved her mouth into a grimace. Damn, what a difference a hundred years made. Her grandmother had been in great demand as both a healer and matchmaker. Her love charms worked, and people paid handsomely for them. Aisha worked her magic with her breeding stock under the proverbial table. Only she knew why her babies were so special, bred for both endurance and speed.

Shaking her head, she covered the remainder of the flagstone path with its runic carvings and let herself inside the house. The scents of sage and hemlock met her nostrils, and she hurried to her small altar. Tonight was the third—and last—night of her ritual. Feeling foolish, she lit a red candle scented with mint and anise and shut her eyes.

Bright the Flame.

Bright the Fire.

Red is the color of my heart's desire.

Aisha repeated the incantation three times, visualizing Liam behind her closed lids. Liam with his curling copper locks, emerald-green eyes, and lanky, broad-shouldered build. That man had an ass on him that was to die for. High and tight and well-muscled. She'd lusted after him for months, but flirting hadn't gained her more than a quick smile before he strode off to attend to something.

"Yeah, nothing normal did the trick," she muttered, "so here I am, sunk into my witchy ways."

She opened her eyes and rolled them. So far as she knew, Liam kept to himself. Maybe he preferred boys, but she didn't think so. Gay men activated a certain frequency of her magic, and he came through as hetero, pure and simple. With a final recitation of her spell, this time in Gaelic, she blew out the candle. The die was cast. No red-blooded male should be able to resist her after that incantation, and she'd find out tomorrow if she'd done any good.

Or the next day. In theory, Liam should move heaven and earth to chase her down, but she had a feeling things might not play out quite that way. Mostly because, he might not be human.

She'd caught glimpses of what may have been magic clinging to him, but it could have been wishful thinking on her part. Aisha strode through the downstairs of her modest home. One large room, it consisted of many floor-to-ceiling bookshelves jammed with magical tomes and scrolls. One end of the downstairs contained an old Wedgewood cookstove, a fridge, and a generous pantry overflowing with dried herbs and home-canned bounty from her garden. The other end held leather furniture and a battered oaken table with four chairs in need of repair. She had electricity but preferred candlelight or kerosene lanterns. A ladder led to the loft where she slept. A lean-to off the kitchen held an old clawfoot bathtub, a commode, and a sink. The bathroom was an add-on since this house had been built over a hundred years before. A combination of spit, elbow grease, and magic kept it standing.

Nothing fancy, but it was comfortable. More importantly, it was hers. No mortgage. No one to answer to. She'd inherited the ranch house, along with the horses, from her mother, who'd taken over from her grandma. Witchiness was passed through women, from one to the next in line. Male children sometimes had power, but never the good kind. Most were weak as yesterday's used-up dishwater and abandoned what magic they had long before hitting adulthood.

At least they didn't have her problems blending in with humankind. For all practical intents and purposes, they *were* human.

Not so for the small percentage of male witches born with destructive magic. At least their proclivities were obvious almost from birth. Warlocks kept to themselves, living in a hidden compound somewhere north of the Arctic Circle. She'd asked a lot of questions, but that was as close as she'd come to an answer about them or their secret society. She assumed someone ferried them to the northlands—and made certain they remained there—but how that happened was anyone's guess.

She poured herself a glass of homemade elderberry brandy and settled into a creased-leather easy chair, pulling an afghan across her lap. Soft and creamy, the woolen folds tucked around her, cradling her body. Her grannie had knitted that afghan, and she missed her.

Aisha sipped the brandy, enjoying the burst of summer brilliance the berry concoction created in her mouth. Crafted with magic like everything else around her, the liquor reminded her of family and love, hearth and home. She blew out a sad breath. Living with humans, trying to blend in, cost a whole lot. Her grannie and mom were still very much alive, but not anywhere close. Not aging normally—never mind not dying for several hundred years—carried a stiff price. She hadn't faced moving on. Not yet, but the day would come eventually just like it did for all witches.

She tightened her grip on the glass and then set it on a nearby table before she shattered the hand-blown crystal. Before she could leave Stillwater and join her witch family, she had to produce a child. Someone who could pick up the banner and care for the horses that were part and parcel of her birthright. Aisha drew breath all the way to the bottom of her lungs before blowing it out.

Her spell to lure Liam was admittedly self-serving, but she had to have sex to create a child. No guarantees her offspring would be female, either. So she might have to go through more than one pregnancy. Everything had to happen over the next few years too. She'd spent her life in Stillwater, which meant everyone in town knew she was north of thirty. Pregnancies happened to women in their thirties but were damned rare after that.

What if Liam was magical, and her spell backfired? Some combinations weren't good bets, and she'd jumped blindly down Alice's rabbit hole when she set her sights on him.

Aisha slogged more brandy down, nearly draining

the glass. Fortified, she lurched to her feet and returned to the small altar where she practiced magic. What she was about to do wasn't precisely forbidden, but nor was it first-line magic.

She switched the red candle for an ivory pillar fragrant with pine, lit it, and chanted, swaying with her words. The air around her developed an electric charge, prickling her skin and drying the saliva in her mouth to sharp clods of mucus. She straightened, staring at the shimmering, glowing space in front of her.

As she expected, her grandmother came into view. Silver hair cascaded to her knees, and she focused shrewd hazel eyes on Aisha. Eyes uncannily like her own. Victoria Colewright crossed her arms beneath her breasts. "Well? This best be good, granddaughter. Have you gotten yourself into a right mess and can't find your way back out again?"

Aisha stood straighter. "You might say that. I cast one of your love charms, but I didn't do much research ahead of time, and—"

Victoria didn't wait for her to finish. "You want me to give you a rundown on the one you have your eye on?"

"Something like that." Aisha kept her gaze trained on the apparition floating in the air a few feet away. It was good to see her grandmother. All crust and bluster, but with a no-nonsense approach that appealed to Aisha's sensibilities. Now wasn't the time to appear cowed or deferential.

"Well." Victoria crooked two gnarled fingers. "My mind reading skills aren't all that sharp in my astral form. I need a name."

Feeling foolish, Aisha swallowed hard, a neat trick as dry as her mouth was. "Of course. It's Liam Fiontan. He's—"

"Ha! I know that one. You may have bitten off a wee bit more than you bargained for, granddaughter. You say you've finished the casting?"

"'Fraid so."

"Why didn't you summon me sooner, for once in your life?"

"Because you always give me nine kinds of hell for not solving my own problems. Grannie. You have to say more than that." Aisha smothered annoyance tinged with apprehension. What had she signed on for?

Victoria narrowed her eyes and angled her head to one side, regarding Aisha. After a pause so long, Aisha wanted to reach through her spell and shake her grandmother, Victoria said, "No. I don't have to say another word. And I'm not going to. You got yourself into this. I trust you'll find a way out."

Anger rushed through her in a white-hot tide.

Before she got hold of her temper, Aisha made a dive for her grandmother's projection, clawing at the air. Her leap was stellar, but she landed belly first on the dusty floorboards, wind knocked out of her.

"None of that, my dear." With a finger shake followed by a snort, Victoria vanished in a shower of silvery sparks.

"Goddamn you!" Aisha rolled to a sit and shook her fists at air still glistening with leftover magic. Her heart pounded hard, and she panted, working to draw air into lungs that felt as if a five-hundred-pound giant perched on her chest.

A strident meow followed by scratches at the kitchen door drove her to her feet and across the room. Of course, the cat would want in. It had belonged to her grandmother originally and would have sensed the old witch's presence.

"Hold on," Aisha called and yanked the door open.

Hector strode in, tail held high. Coal black and at least twenty pounds, he was large as cats went. He glanced her way with odd eyes, one blue, one green, and growled as only a pissed-off tomcat could.

"Yes. She was here," Aisha agreed.

Mrroowww. Swish. Swish.

"I'm sure if she'd stayed longer, she'd have hunted you down." Aisha tried for a reassuring note even though this wasn't a cat who craved anything normal.

Hector strode to his empty dish and glared daggers at her.

Now didn't seem the time to remind him of the rich mouse population roaming the ranch. She grabbed a sack of kitty chow and poured some into his dish. Hector focused on his food, ignoring her now that she'd done as he wished.

Of all the creatures to end up immortal, or damned close to it, why'd Grannie choose the bloody, fucking cat?

Aisha knew better than to voice thoughts like that aloud. If any animal understood human speech, it was Hector. Giving him a wide berth, she plopped back into the leather chair she'd vacated earlier. Her grandmother knew Liam by name, which might mean one of the many books in this house held information.

"Yeah, but I'd at least need a starting place," she muttered. If her charm worked, it would happen fast. She wouldn't have months to cull through her witchy library hunting for clues to Liam's identity.

Enlightenment arrived in an untidy rush; she slapped her forehead, annoyed by what a dolt she'd been. She was making this far more difficult than need be. She could simply ask him who he was, what type of magic he possessed.

Worst thing that would happen is he'd decide she

was a few cards short of a deck—before the charm took over and he screwed her silly.

The more she thought about a direct approach, the better she liked it. If he sought her out, as she expected he would, she'd swathe them in spells and mention her grannie knew him. Maybe it would be sufficient to loosen his tongue. She'd have to disclose her magical pedigree, but now that she knew he was some iteration of magic wielder too, perhaps it wasn't as big a risk as all that.

She looked longingly at the brandy bottle, but it wasn't a good idea. She needed her wits about her, not a fuzzy brain. With all the finesse of a left-end tackle, Hector flew over one of her shoulders and catapulted into her lap, digging his claws in to stabilize his landing.

"Ouch!" Aisha focused a quick jab of power at the cat's razor-sharp claws. He hissed but otherwise ignored her efforts to displace him. It was rare for Hector to demand anything of her beyond food. Usually, she was good at picking information out of animal minds, but his had always been closed to her probing.

Aisha began in a logical spot. "You miss her, huh?"

A deep, rolling meow burst from the cat.

"Yeah, I'd love it if she and Mom were still here." Aisha took a chance and stroked his head. Normally, attempts on her part to mollify him ended up with him either biting her hand or taking a swipe at her eyes.

Unbelievably, Hector leaned into her touch. After one more plaintive meow, he switched to purring. Aisha's mouth fell open. The cat had never warmed to her mother or her. After Victoria had faked her death and moved to points unknown, Aisha had caught her mother grumbling about the cat many times. When she'd asked why they didn't find another family for the unruly feline, her mother's tart reply skirted the issue. Aisha's take-home message had been that magical creatures picked their abodes, not the reverse.

"What's all this about?" Aisha kept her question light, conversational, and kept stroking the cat.

A series of disjointed sounds blatted through her head.

"Whoa. Are you trying to talk with me?" She scratched under Hector's chin, not expecting an answer. She communicated telepathically with the horses, a magical undertaking that began before they were born. It was why her horses were so special. They listened to her, trusted her, and for the most part followed her direction.

In that regard, the large tomcat sitting in her lap had almost nothing in common with her Arabians. No listening. No trust. And most assuredly no direction following.

Hector purred louder, the rumble soothing and thrilling at the same time. She'd always loved animals, from the laciest butterfly to dolphins and elephants. One of her dreams was to travel to Africa and see if any of the big cats or monkeys or other game animals would offer her a peek into their minds.

Discordant notes rioted through her head again. Aisha switched to telepathy to provide a template for the cat. *"Slow down. I'm not going anywhere."*

Hector skinned his upper lip back, showing yellowed fangs. She stroked his head, but he shook her off. Relieved and disappointed by turns that the cat she'd known all the years of her life was back, she raised her hands, palms outward. "I'm ready whenever you are, Hec."

"Victoria witch here." The cat's words were garbled, but easy enough to understand.

"Yes," Aisha agreed, blown away her gambit worked, and the cat was actually talking to her. *"My grandmother was here, but you already knew that."*

"Why not here now?"

How to answer that? *"It's my fault. I became angry when she refused to answer a question."*

Hector extended his claws, kneading her thigh. *"Bring her back. Now."*

Heat trickled down her leg. Blood from the cat's claws. *"I'd love to,"* she replied, *"but Victoria does what she pleases, not what I want."* Aisha steadied herself, prepared for another, more vicious onslaught from Hector's claws. It didn't come.

Instead, he hopped off her lap and sat facing her, tail curved around his front feet in the way of cats. His gaze skewered her; Aisha made an effort to hold her mind open, so he'd know she wasn't hiding anything. Pinpricks of primitive magic poked behind her eyes as the cat probed her mind. They weren't quite as bad as his claws had been.

Time dribbled past. Aisha quirked her mouth into half a smile. "Are we done for tonight?"

Hector leapt into the air, executed a one-eighty, and stalked toward the front door. Aisha sent a beam of power to open it, and the cat sauntered into the night. Interesting that it could talk, but it was a creature of magic, which meant it might well have other talents she didn't appreciate—or know about.

"Yeah. Because I never looked for them."

Maybe Victoria had left it to spy first on her mother and then on her. That might explain why Hector was so out of sorts...

Aisha slumped against the worn chair. The concept of the cat as some sort of arcane spy was beyond ridiculous. Her thighs ached from kitty-imposed cuts and scrapes. She marshaled healing magic, sending it to her injured spots, while replaying the conversation with her grandmother. The old woman had seemed more amused than worried, which probably meant Liam didn't pose a threat. If he did, Victoria would still be here, or more likely, she'd be pounding truth into Liam, and that truth would include never laying so much as a finger on her granddaughter.

Or else.

Aisha had heard plenty of "or elses" from her grannie. She'd never wanted to dig any deeper. If Victoria was spun out enough about something to issue a threat, it was time to sit up and take notice, not write it off as idle posturing.

She missed Victoria, and her mother, Charlotte. More than that, she missed being part of a family. Witches packed up in covens, or they had a century or two ago. Not anymore. Concealing your status as a magical being got in the way of belonging to covens or any other magical societies. Her mind pedaled in circles that went nowhere, and she recognized a familiar spot. One where it made sense to cut bait and stop trying to force order out of anything.

Tomorrow was soon enough. Today was done—if she was smart enough to accept it and shut off her brain.

Weariness washed over her in waves. She stumbled to the kitchen sink and cupped her hands beneath the flow of water, sluicing it over her face. She gave her teeth a lick and a promise with her willow wand toothbrush and climbed the ladder to the loft. After stopping at the bootjack long enough to lever her feet out of her boots, she crossed the open beam loft to the same featherbed her mother and grandmother had slept in.

She'd been born in this bed, as had her mother. The power of her family, of the Colewrights, rose around her as she lay down. Usually, she lit a candle and read a bit. Not tonight. Closing eyes that felt hot and filled with grit, she plumped a down pillow beneath her head. A kaleidoscope of forms and colors danced behind her lids. Cats. Horses. Dragons.

The last drew a soft snort from between her lips. Even she, magical as she was, knew dragons hadn't been seen for centuries. Too damned bad. She'd have loved to lay eyes on one before they vanished from the face of the earth. Rumors had spread fast and furious among the witches of yore, but no one disputed dragons were well and truly gone, having left Earth for somewhere they could fly free.

"Free," she muttered. "I'm so far from free, I may as well wear shackles."

Not that she didn't love her horses, but she was chained at the ankles to this ranch as surely as if she wore manacles. Normally, it didn't bother her, but tonight she wanted more. Craved a world where she wasn't knee-deep in horseshit and horsey connivery every single day. Far from subtle, horses were dogged, rarely giving ground until they got what they wanted. It was one trait they shared with the cat.

"*Watch what you ask for,*" an inner voice whispered.

A chill slid down Aisha's spine just before sleep whisked her away.

CHAPTER 3

A flare of witchy magic jabbed Liam between the shoulder blades as he bent over the Chevy's bed, gathering the tools of his trade. Hot. Pagan. Wild. The sensation slid down his body like a naked vixen with a million fingers stroking his sensitive spots. The imaginary fingers fueled lust until breath caught in his throat and his cock shot to attention.

Not giving in to the intense desire tantalizing him was almost impossible. Almost, but he could manage it. If he curled his fingers around his burning, aching erection, he'd come the moment he touched himself.

And then the magic bombarding him would snatch up the scent of his semen, and he'd be lost.

It was that pesky witch. Pretty much had to be. She'd been making eyes at him for months. Not that she wasn't striking. Tall for a woman, she had broad shoulders and powerful legs, probably from all the time she spent astride a horse. Hair the color of summer-wheat sheaves rolled down her back to waist level, and unusual hazel eyes with tip-tilted corners nested above high cheekbones and a strong, square jaw.

A visual of her astride not one of her Arabian stallions but him as a dragon made it tough to breathe. He fisted one hand and brought it down hard on the pickup bed. Pain stoked his arousal, and his cock jerked against his belly. If his trousers rubbed against him, it would push him past caring.

"Bad decision." He gritted the words into the dark silence of his yard.

The vixen of a witch had been trying to seduce him for a long time. He hoped she'd given up, but apparently she'd only been taking a break before casting her dirty, sneaky spells.

Another blast of power caught him mid-chest, turning his nipples into red-hot points of need. His entire body transformed into a sexually charged mass of protoplasm, the desire as pervasive as if he were caught up in the dragon mating ritual. Not that he'd ever engaged in that particular aerial dance, but he'd borne witness to other dragons, their lust so palpable it made him horny for months. It was how he'd ended up seducing his cousin's wife.

When he'd pled his case, the dragon council had

told him lust wasn't much of an excuse for his behavior. As a fully matured dragon shifter, he was expected to have better control over his desires. Goddammit to hell. All the sexual imagery wasn't helping. His balls tightened, snugging closer to his body. Panic followed.

Did it count if he came spontaneously? Would any orgasm, no matter how it happened, bind him to sex with the witch?

"I cannot sleep with her." Liam was back to talking out loud. "If I do, she'll figure out what I am. Witches are notorious blabbermouths.

"Aye, but I was considering leaving Stillwater anyway. What's the harm in a wee tumble afore I go?"

A low groan burst past his lips. Not only had he answered himself, the harm was obvious. Once he bedded the witch, when and how he left would be up to her. Giving in to her spell would mark him as weaker than her magically, and she'd think she could lead him around by the nose.

The thought was like a bucket of ice water. No fucking, bloody way was a dragon shifter weaker than a witch. Even as an exile, he sat at the pinnacle of shifterdom. Never mind that even a garden-variety bird shifter should wield stronger magic than most witches.

Galvanized into considering something other than his cock, still throbbing like a second heart between his legs, he shouldered his pack, grabbed his hardware belt, and schlepped everything into the miner's cabin he called home. Neat by nature—all dragons were, else the elements in their hoards would get away from them—Liam returned everything to its customary spot.

His truck was the one spot where tidiness slid, but he mucked it out periodically.

When he'd taken over the shack, it had been decrepit, one side falling in, and the roof not much better than a sieve. After a surreptitious trip through the county records building that assured him no long-lost relatives were likely to show up to claim the cabin, he'd resurrected what there was of it. It might not be much with a single main room and a bedroom in back, but it was his. The kitchen sink had a pump affair that brought cold water from a nearby creek. Heating water was such simple magic he'd never bothered to repair the water heater.

He'd had an electric line installed, chinked the holes between the logs, and repaired the roof with new sheets of corrugated metal. The place was cozy and weatherproof. The closest thing he'd had to a home since being booted from Xara.

He closed the cabinet where he kept climbing hardware. Everything was put away. The enforced activity had rescued him from the brink of spilling his seed spontaneously, but his balls ached. At least the witch's onslaught seemed finished. If that was her best shot, it was laughable.

I shouldn't underestimate her. She got me pretty good.

Nah. Only because it was a stealth attack, he answered himself.

He left the cabin at a fast trot, headed for the mineshaft a hundred yards away. It was a lot of trouble to go to just to jack off, but he'd seal his presence deep in the mine with his own brand of magic. Once he did, he'd be invisible to her witchy charms, and it would be safe to indulge himself.

He hoped.

The wisest course would be to go to bed. His hard-on would be gone before morning, but he'd never been one to opt for safe courses. Liam plunged into the mineshaft, engaging his drakish eyesight to see in the dark. As if it knew what he was about, his cock pushed against the front of his pants, eager for him to wrap his fingers around its length.

"Not yet, but soon." His breathing, which had begun to normalize, quickened again.

Two more twists in the tunnel, and he came to the cave where he'd sequestered his hoard. The gold and gems sparkled invitingly. For a brief moment, a different kind of lust took over.

Liam spun in a wide circle, scattering power as he

went, until he'd sealed off the cave. With uncharacteristic caution, he tested his ward from the dirt floor to the rocky ceiling, not finding any weak places.

Satisfied, he knelt next to his pile of loot, hollowed out a place to sit, and unzipped his jeans. His unruly appendage all but jumped into his hand. If he gripped himself hard, a single stroke might bring him off, but he'd gone to a lot of trouble for this opportunity, and he'd be damned if it would be over almost before it began.

He ran a finger from base to tip, feeling his cock shudder beneath his touch. Another fingertip teased its way up the other side. So far, so good. He'd been afraid the witch, Aisha, would inveigle her way into his mind. If that happened, he'd have to quit, no matter how aroused he was. It would mean her spell had somehow penetrated his ward.

He licked two fingers and swirled them around the head of his cock where the skin was velvet-smooth. Heat spiraled outward from his belly, and he shut his eyes. Dragons winging through purple-hazed air danced through his visual field.

Mating dragons.

Satisfaction bit deep. What better fantasy to spin? It beat the hell out of imagining yanking Aisha's riding pants to her knees, bending her over a hay bale, and driving himself into her.

Not that that didn't get him going too.

"Dragons, back to the dragons." His heartbeat sped up still more, and he'd wrapped a hand around his shaft without realizing what he was about.

The dragons—a black male and a red female—obligingly returned. The male's cock was engorged, curved against the scales of his belly, and he bellowed his desire. The smaller red female did a flip midair that exposed her slit, the lips puffy and distended. The musky reek of dragon heat curled around Liam, and he stroked his shaft.

In his vision, he was dragon, not human, and his cock so large, it took both taloned forefeet to hold himself.

The female did another aerial somersault to display her sex. This time, the black bugled hotly and flew after her. At first, it appeared she might outfly him —smaller and more maneuverable, she could have except she wanted to be caught. The black drew even and dropped atop her from above, grabbing onto her shoulders with his forelegs. The next part happened fast, but then it always did with dragonkind.

The black jackknifed his hindquarters and drove his more-than-ready erection into the female beneath him. She squealed and writhed, clearly lost in ecstasy. The black thrust into her, hard and sure.

Liam pumped into his hand, holding his full-to-bursting erection as tight as he could. Breath tinged with flames shot from his mouth as he frigged himself, sunk in lust so pervasive his vision clouded over with hunger. He'd time this, goddammit. He'd come when the black did.

The red dragon shrieked her delight. She was driving her hindquarters back and upward, meeting the black stroke for stroke. Fire shot from both their mouths. Liam inhaled heat and lust and need.

He pushed his other hand between his legs, forefinger hunting for the magical spot just behind his balls. It pulsed beneath his touch when he found it. Eyes closed, head thrown back, he frigged himself harder, faster. Semen boiled from his balls, exploding in gouts of white heat.

The dragons forgotten, he lost himself in waves of lust rolling through him. Once didn't come close to slaking his need, so he kept right on jacking himself, knowing he could come again, and the second time would be even hotter than the first.

Liam lost track of everything for a long time. When he came back to himself, he lay in a sweat-soaked heap atop his hoard, surrounded by a satiated haze and the salt-tang of his semen. At least Aisha hadn't invaded his indulgence. Or if she had, he hadn't noticed, which had to mean he'd won. His magic trumped hers. He'd outwitted her spell by hiding inside his own.

He curled to a sit, making a disgusted sound. Dragons did not hide. He'd merely done what was necessary to evade her underhanded ploy to seduce him. Nothing more. Nothing less.

If she'd been human, he'd probably have taken her up on her flirty offers. But she wasn't. Anything he said would reveal he had magic, and then they'd edge around to questions like, which kind? If she had any level of power at all, she'd figure out what he was without much effort. Tough to hide power as strong as his.

A quote from Gide marched across his mind. Something about straight gates and narrow paths leading to temptation. Better to walk away than tempt fate.

"But I need a mate," he muttered.

"A mate, not a witch," he answered himself.

Liam got to his feet and released the magic holding his ward in place. Once it was gone, he walked slowly uphill to the mineshaft's entrance and out into the chilly night. It felt marvelous on his overheated skin. He whistled a jaunty Gaelic folk tune as he covered the distance to the house and let himself inside.

Now that his lust was taken care of, he was hungry,

and he made himself a sandwich and filched a beer from the fridge. He didn't know much about how witchy charms worked, but she'd be in for a hell of a surprise when he didn't show up on her doorstep with the mating light burning.

The image made him laugh so hard, he choked on a bite of chicken sandwich and washed the problem piece down with a slug of beer. No human could have resisted her, that was certain.

The implication hit him like a fist to the midsection, and he set the rest of his food back on the counter. She'd figure out quick enough he was immune to her spell, and she'd put two and two together. She might not know what he was right now, but she'd ascertain he had to be *something*.

Crap. Maybe his plans to pull up stakes and leave were more prophetic than he'd believed driving down the mountain road earlier this evening.

"I'm being an idiot. Who would she tell even if she did figure things out? Beyond that, no one would believe her. Dragons left earth eons ago." With a huffing snort, he picked the remains of the sandwich back up, determined to finish it.

Insofar as he could tell, she was the only witch in Stillwater. It had surprised him. They usually hung out in covens, or they had in the Old Country. Out of all the backwater places where he'd remained for longer than it took to stop in at the local watering hole for a brew, Stillwater was the only one with more than one or two magic-wielders. At first, he'd assumed he'd stumbled onto a secret den, but the shifters and Fae and the lone witch were just as closemouthed about what they were here as they'd been everywhere else.

When he let himself think about how magic wielders had turned into pariahs, it made him angry. Humans were a tight-assed bunch of prudes. Anything unfamiliar scared them. They seemed to have gotten past the burnings and hangings they'd relied on a hundred years back, but it didn't mean they wanted a wolf shifter living next door.

Not that they knew about, anyway.

He shrugged and tilted the beer back. Hell, he could barely solve his own problems. No way could he take on more global ones. Besides, his tenure here was drawing to a close. Maybe. Once he returned to Xara, he could give a crap less what happened with the magical tribe on Earth.

A muted yip from his cell phone drew his attention to the battered plastic case with its annoying electronics within. He considered ignoring it, but the caller ID said, SAR.

If Search and Rescue was calling him, they must need help. He wasn't officially a part of their organization, mostly because the meetings bored him to tears and he didn't have time for all their practice sessions, but he had told them he'd make himself available if they needed climbers.

He'd given his word, which meant he had to pick up. Clicking the accept icon, he said, "Aye?"

"Thank fucking God. I was afraid you weren't there," a male voice blurted.

"And you might be?" Liam pressed, smothering irritation he'd let honor win out over common sense. With his uncharitable feelings about humans, not picking up might have been the better choice.

"Andy. You know from the local SAR group. We met when—"

"I recall," Liam cut in. "What do you need?"

"We've got a man stranded five hundred feet from the ground and three hundred from the top on The Spider. He's scared out of his wits, and—"

"Why can't he downclimb? He got himself up there."

"Yes. Yes. But he's in over his head. Called in a rescue with his PLB. Anyway, it's a dicey wall. You know it. You hold the speed record for solo-climbing it without protection. It's why I called you."

"What precisely were you hoping I could do, mate?"

"Climb down to him and calm him. Maybe top rope him up from there."

Liam shut his eyes for a moment, visualizing the wall. Not much of anywhere to top rope from. Not for a three-hundred-foot stretch."

"You still there, Liam?" Andy's words held a thin, strained note. It didn't take magic to hear he was afraid the hapless climber was a goner.

"Aye, mate. I'm thinking. Do you have anyone but me in mind?"

"You were my first choice—"

"Not what I meant. Would I be by myself, or did you scare up a few other climbers for this mission?"

"Three more, plus a ground crew. Does that mean you're in?"

Liam blew out a long, breath. "Aye. I'm in, but only so long as this is my operation. I don't want to end up arguing with someone who thinks they know that wall better than me."

"No arguments. How soon can you be there?"

"An hour. I have to pack a couple of gear bags before I leave."

"See you there. And, Liam?"

"Aye?"

"Thanks. The man who's stuck, he's my brother-in-law. My sister is hysterical, and I don't want to face her or their kids if Jerry bites it. As it is, they blame me for him climbing."

Aha! The plot thickens.

"Don't mention it. See you soon." Liam disconnected. If humans weren't such assholes, he could simply shift to his dragon form and scoop Jerry off the wall.

Fifteen minutes later, he backed out of his driveway headed for the popular local wall. Popular, but rarely climbed because of its complexity. He offered Jerry points for guts. Too bad they'd failed him at the crux point of the route. Liam ground his teeth. PLBs, personal locator beacons, were a scourge. A blight on the landscape. They gave you a backdoor out, so you didn't try very hard.

Or at all.

Look on the bright side, he told himself. Tonight was an opportunity to climb, something he loved more than almost anything except flying. He fished out his phone and hit redial.

Andy picked up on the first ring. "You didn't change your mind?"

"No, mate. I never do that. Just wanted to clarify. I'm driving the route up the back and going on foot from there to the top of the pitch. Faster getting to him that way than up from the bottom."

"We'll be there when you arrive."

"Good." Liam rattled off a series of instructions. He'd had time to think through the best way to approach Jerry while he tossed gear into backpacks.

Andy whistled long and low. "Brilliant. Gutsy. Never would have thought of that combination, but it should work."

"Not should. If everyone does their work properly, it will."

IT WAS two hours past dawn when Liam made it back to his pickup. He'd had to hit Jerry with a shot of magic to calm him down enough to get him moving. Once the man was clipped into slings and ascenders, he'd scooted up ropes snaking along the face like a champ. He'd even taken the spot where he had to switch ropes in stride.

Of course, Liam had been right next to him the whole time, free climbing. And the last fifty feet were simple class-four moves. Jerry was feeling pretty good by then and finished that bit on his own. He'd thanked Liam profusely and told him a check for five thousand bucks would materialize in his office the following day.

Liam deferred, but Jerry had insisted. He ran the real estate office in town. Well-known and well-liked, he'd be great for Liam's guide business.

Yeah. If I stick around.

He tossed gear into the back of the pickup preparing to drive into Stillwater. He often went out to eat, and this morning he'd decided on breakfast in one of the two town cafés.

Shaking his head, he lumbered into his pickup. One of the best things about this whole SAR saga was he hadn't thought about Aisha once. A gout of smoke blew past his lips. He'd bet every ounce of gold in his hoard she'd thought of nothing but him since she cast her presumptuous spell.

He'd adopt his usual polite demeanor if he ran into her. Something like that was bound to blow her away. She'd have the devil's own time sorting through where she'd gone wrong.

Chuckling, he backed the truck around, put it in low gear, and slipped and slid down the steep, rocky track toward town.

CHAPTER 4

Aisha herded the horses into the lower pasture as dawn was breaking. She mucked stalls and spread fresh rice hulls before tossing hay and oats in everyone's buckets. A whistle combined with a shot of magic brought her group of charges cantering back. Every morning was the same, and she never had to convince them to show up for breakfast. A few times, she'd gotten sidetracked, and the horses had returned on their own with head tosses and annoyed whinnies.

They were her first priority, and no one knew it better than them.

They trotted into the barn, heads high, tails swishing. She grabbed a handful of mane before Butch, her favorite, got lost in his food bucket. "Want to go for a ride, bud?"

A quick glance into his mind showed his

dilemma. He loved to run with her on his back, but he also loved oats. Before she got any serious pushback, she vaulted onto his back and wheeled him around. Once they left the corral circling the barn, she shut the gate with magic to keep the rest of her babies in one spot.

Not that they ever went far. Magic linked them to this place as surely as it bound her. She urged Butch into an easy canter, enjoying the feel of the horse's powerful muscles moving between her thighs. She always rode bareback. No saddle. No bridle. Not even a blanket. When the day came she couldn't control her mounts with magic, she should pack it in.

Big words. Hope I don't end up choking on them.

She was halfway to town before she realized what she was up to, and it brought her up short. Her spell from the previous night was in ascendance, and she was on her way to town to hunt for Liam.

Not just hunt for him, either. He should be ripe for the plucking about now, and she was more than ready. Maybe she was reacting to the sheer maleness of the horse between her legs or its enticing motion, but desire beat a path through her, heating her blood.

Once unleashed, lust pummeled her until it took all her self-control not to jam a hand between her legs. The state she was in, the lightest touch would topple her over the edge.

Focus! She fairly screamed the word into her mind and set about communicating with her frisky steed.

Butch was having a grand old time, so it took another half mile before her suggestions to stop—followed by threats of what would happen if he kept thumbing his hooves at her—had any effect.

Maybe bridles weren't such a bad invention after all.

He stamped and pawed, clearly furious with her for spoiling his fun. Born and bred to run free in the desert, he viewed them as a team, which meant he should have an equal say in their activities...

She withdrew from his mind, knowing he'd be further outraged by her snooping through his thoughts. "Time to go home," she cooed brightly.

Her words were met with a derisive snort. He planted both front feet and laid his ears back. She pushed harder with magic, but it backfired. The stallion reared, hitting the ground hard enough to rattle her bones when he landed.

"Stop that!" she shouted. To hell with magic. She'd revert to good old reminding him who the hell the alpha was in their herd.

He reared again, sashaying his hindquarters around at the same time.

Damn! He was trying to unseat her. That was so not going to happen. She wrapped her arms as far as she could get them around his neck and tightened her legs. The motion accentuated the contact between her girl bits and Butch's back, but she'd moved from lust to anger. The stallion bucked and reared. He crab-walked, all the while braying a challenge.

Aisha clung to him, while she buried her anger six-feet under. The horse would latch onto it and make this whole mess that much worse. Once she had her fury under control, she fed soothing thoughts into his mind, told him he was the best horse ever, that he didn't have to do this, that she'd always love him even if he didn't prove his alpha-readiness.

She was sweating, despite the day not being much over forty-five, and breathing hard by the time Butch got over his snit. This road was never busy but thank the goddess no one had driven by. They'd have stopped, she was sure of it, and laughed their fool heads off.

Then she'd never have regained the upper hand. Horses were proud. Laughing at them was the wrong approach since it pushed them even further into stubborn-land.

"That's better," she purred as his jerky rebellion transformed into walking in an easy circle. She pressed her right leg against him, hoping to turn him toward home, but he resisted. Hoping to avoid another half hour of fighting fifteen hundred pounds of determined stallion, she ceded control.

Just this once, she told herself.

Recognizing he'd won, Butch tossed his head and took off toward town. What the hell was it about Stillwater that drew him? Or was he as snared in her love charm as she was. Left to their own devices, horses would fuck merrily for days, as long as the mare remained in heat.

Stallions were dogged—and tireless. Aisha redirected her thoughts. Too bad her sex life couldn't be as simple and uncomplicated as a horse's.

She scooted forward, adjusting her position to a slightly more comfortable spot. Maybe she'd pissed away enough time, Liam would be long gone from town by now. He favored The Rise and Grind Café for breakfast, but it must be ten o'clock. She wanted to find him, but not this way.

Not when her spell was driving her, and she didn't trust herself not to rip off her clothes and spread her legs in the middle of Main Street. A snort rippled past her lips at the visual. The townsfolk liked her now, but she could blow that to kingdom come if she indulged in those kinds of shenanigans.

The word shenanigans held her grandmother's inflection. Such an old-fashioned word. Aisha blew out a breath. Her breathing was back to normal, the sweat that had coated her face and trunk nearly dry. She probably didn't smell all that swift, but she couldn't do much to correct that until she got home and jumped in the shower.

Thinking about Victoria dragged last night's conversation front and center. What in the name everything unholy did she know about Liam? Her crabby old cow of a grandmother had sounded almost smug, which meant she knew him in an up-close and personal way.

It also meant she knew what kind of magic ran through him. Aisha screwed her face into a thoughtful expression. The cat wanted Victoria to return for unknown feline reasons of its own. Would that be sufficient incentive to lure her for long enough to have a decent conversation? It didn't take a witch's intuition to know her grannie held information. Data Aisha needed before proceeding.

What if having sex with Liam would spawn a permanent bond? Something she couldn't unravel if she tried? Unease poked holes in her lust but didn't obliterate it.

Not entirely.

She'd reached the sprawling ranches dotting Stillwater's outskirts. A couple of cars rattled past.

The drivers waved. She waved back.

Still determined to run the show, Butch turned

hard right, heading for the feed store. "Oh so that's it, huh?" she teased him. He tossed his head, making his tawny mane glitter in sunlight filtering through thickening clouds. If the sky was any harbinger, she'd be riding home in a downpour.

Unless she sat it out in town. Rain in the Sierras could be intense, but it rarely lasted long. The horse stopped in front of Stillwater Feed and Vet Supply and craned his head around until he made eye contact.

Aisha tossed a leg over his back and jumped down. Grabbing a handy bridle from the end of the hitching rack, she slid it over Butch's head in one practiced motion and secured a rope to the clip, tying the other end around a nearby post. A shudder rippled through the stallion as it sank in that playtime was over.

She swatted his withers and strolled into the feed store.

Aaron Middleton looked up from where he sat in front of a screen. Gray hair fell untidily around his seamed face, and his brown eyes were kind as he smiled her way. He wore his usual: jeans, scuffed cowboy boots, and a faded Western shirt. A green bandana looped around his neck. "What'll it be, Aisha? Gosh, I just dropped off enough feed to hold even your crew for a few more days."

"Yeah. I know you did, but I gave Butch his head,

and this is where he ended up." She turned her hands palms up.

"He did, eh?" Aaron pushed to his feet and ducked down an aisle, returning with a mash pack. "Mind if I give this to him?" He raised a gray brow. "Gotta reward the little man for helping drive business where it belongs."

A laugh rippled from her. "Sure. He's scarcely what I'd call little, but he'll love the attention. You know how Butch is."

"Indeed, I do." Aaron strode out the door with the peculiar gait common to men who spent much of their lives astride a horse.

While he was gone, she grabbed an order sheet and scribbled on it, noting her next order and when she wanted it delivered. Consulting a calendar on the wall, she saw it was November 6th today. Sheesh, autumn was getting away from her.

Aaron came back through the swinging door, a broad smile illuminating his face. "That's one fine piece of horseflesh out there. You ever want to sell him, I want first dibs."

Aisha chuckled. "That's rich. If you'd asked me an hour ago, I'd have given him to you. He's got an independent streak, that one." She handed her next order to him. "So long as I was here, thought it was easier than phoning it in."

Aaron snatched the paper from her and laid it atop his desk. "Always a pleasure, Aisha. Hell, I still miss your mom and grannie." He shook his head. "Sorry. That probably wasn't smart of me. No reason to make you sad."

She laid a hand over his. "Not sad. They both had amazing lives. See you next time."

"Next time," he echoed as she walked out the door. Her mother and grandma had gone to a whole lot of trouble pretending to die. No reason to tell Aaron she wasn't sad about her female relatives because they were both very much alive and kicking. Just not here.

Butch was still chewing, a blissful expression on his horsey face.

"Good, eh?" She unhooked the lead rope, deciding to borrow the bridle and reins. Aaron wouldn't mind. She'd return them tomorrow when she drove into town. Her next move was ill-advised, but she trotted the length of Main Street with an eye out for Liam's trashed pickup. It wasn't there. Feeling bold, she even checked the alleyways on both sides.

Satisfied she'd escaped a speeding bullet, but sad and empty at the same time, she turned Butch's head toward home. He didn't fight her this time. Maybe the mash did the trick. Today had set a very bad precedent, though. It taught the horse he could go where he wanted with her along as a passenger.

As they trotted toward home, she linked to his mind and planted the suggestion that good horses waited for permission before bolting. He snickered and whinnied, assuring her of his intentions to be the best horse ever. She'd see what a model horse he could be.

"Oh, I'll see, all right," she told him out loud. "You'll be the perfect stallion. Until next time."

He tossed his head, braying equine laughter. He was still chortling, choking on saliva, when they turned onto the long road leading to her ranch. The rain that had threatened was just starting to fall in big, fat drops that landed on her head and ran down her neck and back.

By the time she'd escorted Butch to the locked-in side of the corral and dropped the bridle and reins into the back of her Ford F350 to make sure she wouldn't forget them tomorrow, she was soaked through. The air had developed a prickly aspect, so lightning and thunder weren't far behind. As if her thoughts were prophetic, a jagged golden fork split the black clouds overhead, followed by the rolling boom of thunder.

Aisha ran for the house, stopping in the laundry room to shuck her wet clothing. She kept peeling layers off until she was down to her underwear, but they were wet too. Deciding she may as well go for a clean sweep, she unhooked her bra and pushed her sodden panties down her legs.

She stood under the shower for a long time, letting hot water pelt her while her mind jumped from topic to topic. From the unruly horse to Liam to whatever secret her grandmother had decided she didn't need to know. By the time she was toweling herself dry, she had the bones of a plan in place.

All she needed was the cat.

Luckily, it didn't prove to be a problem. Once she was dressed in a comfy set of warm, black sweats and her old sheepskin slippers, she walked into the kitchen. Her first bit of bait was the cupboard. She made sure to rattle the latch and slam the can of cat food down on the counter. She tapped the can opener on the can for good measure, and then proceeded to open it.

She considered calling Hector but didn't want to lay it on too thick. The cat was uncannily smart. Maybe he wasn't really a magical cat, but some type of sprite or gnome or changeling who'd adopted cat form. The more she thought about it, the more likely it seemed. If Victoria—or her mother before her—wanted a way to keep tabs on things from beyond their fake graves, what better way than via an innocuous, onsite sentinel?

She was bent over Hector's dish, spooning canned food over his kibbles when the big black cat sashayed through the cat door. She may as well have not been there for all the attention he paid her. Aisha moved aside and tucked the other half of the can into the fridge, dropping the spoon in the sink.

Hector ate hunkered over his dish, growling as if he expected a dozen cats to storm the kitchen and try to steal his food. Aisha resisted the temptation to roll her eyes. Respect was key dealing with any animal, even if this particular animal might be something else entirely.

"I had an idea," she murmured from where she leaned against the kitchen counter. "You wanted Grannie back here, and I've thought about how we could make it happen."

The cat didn't look up right away; he went right on eating.

Aisha dusted her hands together. "All right. If you're not interested, I have chores."

Hector twisted his head and gave her a baleful stare. He ran his tongue over his lips and cast a longing look at the remaining wet food.

"I'm not going to take it away," she reassured him. "I just want to talk."

He turned until he faced her, ears pricked forward. She took it as a good sign. "Grandma likes you. Have you called for her lately?"

Hector shook his head. Feline laughter rocketed through her mind, which didn't make a whole lot of sense.

Aisha squatted so she was close to eye level with

him, and she lowered her voice to a conspiratorial whisper. Cats loved shit like that. They all saw themselves as miniature covert operatives. "If you want her to come back, tell her you have important news. News that won't wait. I bet you anything, she'll come running."

Yeah, and then we can both talk with her.

Hector's feline face took on a disgusted look, as if he'd latched onto a mouse too rotten for even his taste. *"But that's lying,"* he ground into her mind. *"Trickery."*

She forced back a snort. Good to know the cat had principles. Who would have guessed? "Not really," Aisha countered. "You might tell her you're worried about the spell I completed last night. The magic felt wrong to you." She took a measured breath before adding, "You tried to tell her last night, but she was gone too fast."

Power shimmered around the cat. For the blink of an eye, he took on another form, but it was gone so fast she couldn't get a bead on it. "What are you?" The words blitzed out before she had a chance to think better of them.

Alarm rolled off Hector before he spun and ran through his cat door.

"Goddammit!" She pounded a fist on the scarred linoleum.

"Something wrong, dear?" Victoria's honeyed contralto preceded her into the room.

Aisha shot to her feet. "Yeah, Grannie. A whole lot." Before Victoria could pull the same mind-fuck she'd done the previous night, Aisha draped a magical net around both of them. She had questions, and she'd be damned if her grandmother was leaving without answering at least some of them.

CHAPTER 5

"*N*ow, now. No need for Draconian measures," Victoria's words were laced with compulsion.

"Stop that!" Aisha stared her kinswoman straight in the eye.

"I'm sure I have no idea what you're talking about." Victoria thinned her mouth into a harsh line. "Why were you instigating problems?"

"I'm sure I have no idea what you're taking about." Aisha mimicked her grandmother's words down to matching the inflection.

"Oh for the love of the goddess, let's drop this ridiculous game. Why were you encouraging Hector to lie? It wouldn't have done you much good. Contrary to what you believe, the cat isn't particularly fond of me."

"It wasn't a lie. Not exactly." Defensiveness carved

a path through her. Victoria frequently had that effect, mostly because she was a master at grabbing the upper hand and hanging onto it.

"Let's not split hairs. You wanted me back here. I knew that last night." She sent a knowing look down her aquiline nose. Aisha had always hated that look with its combination of superciliousness and mild contempt.

No reason to deny it, so Aisha folded her arms beneath her breasts. "Tell me what you know about Liam."

"Why?"

Aisha ground her teeth. "How about this? If I fuck him, will I live to regret it? You and Mom are always nattering away about me keeping the family line going. I can't do that if I don't have sex."

Victoria spun one hand in a tired circle. "Depends what kind of spawn you want to produce, but no, he's not the best choice."

"Why? What don't I know?"

"Oh, very well." Victoria's nostrils flared. "He's a dragon shifter, and—"

Breath whooshed from Aisha. If a mule had kicked her in the guts, it would have produced much the same effect.

"Oh come now, child. Surely you guessed something was up with him. Otherwise, why pick him and not some garden-variety cowboy? They have dicks too."

"I picked him because I was attracted to him." Aisha tried for dignity but fell short. She felt stupid. Magic called to its own, and she should have known.

Laughter spewed from her grandmother until Aisha wanted to strangle her. When she got hold of herself, she said, "Of course, you'd be 'attracted' to him. He's the most potent magic wielder around here by a good big bunch."

"But," Aisha sputtered, "all the dragons left Earth."

"At least you got something right." Victoria skewered her with one of her looks—again.

Aisha shook her head, hoping for clearer thoughts. "They can't be gone and here at the same time."

"To the best of my knowledge, he's the only one here. He was a bad dragon, and his kin banished him. I believe it was a time-linked eviction, but I don't have details."

Aisha chewed her lower lip. "Which means he's due to leave Earth sometime."

"Smart witch." Victoria patted her arm, ghostly fingers feeling chilly when they connected. "I'll save you the trouble of putting it together. If you bind yourself to him, it means you'll end up leaving too. Dragons have strong ties to their home world. Really strong." She slitted her hazel eyes. "That cannot happen. Someone must be here. On this land. With our horses."

"How come you didn't tell me all this last night?"

Her grannie shrugged. "I hadn't thought things through. Last night, I saw the humorous side, but I kicked it around with your mother, and we decided one of us had to stop you."

"Mmph. I guess I didn't need to co-opt Hector. Or try to. While I'm on that topic, what the hell is he?"

Victoria shook a finger beneath her nose. "Enough classified information for one day."

Aisha strengthened her casting. "What if I said I wouldn't release you until you told me?"

"That would be a big mistake, dearie. A very big mistake. Do you want to be looking over your shoulder for the next century wondering how I'm going to retaliate?"

"Erm. No." Aisha swallowed hard, dropped her hands to her sides, and reeled in her magic. Victoria was more than capable of making good on her threat, and Aisha had enough problems.

"Better." Victoria smiled benignly. "Lovely chat. I'll be on my way."

"But what should I do about my love charm?"

"It'll run its course. You might want to lie low for a few days." Victoria's glistening form took on a liquid aspect before it shimmered into nothingness, leaving Aisha standing dead center in her empty kitchen.

She owed Hector an apology but didn't want to take the time to run him down, so she sent warm thoughts and a clear telepathic invitation to come back inside. He must have been close because he slunk through the cat door and made a beeline for his dish, all without glancing her way.

Water dripped from his luxuriant coat, forming puddles on the floor. She thought about wrapping him in a towel to soak up some of the excess, but she'd done enough damage for one day. He hated it when she touched him. Checking on stew meat she'd taken out of the freezer earlier in the day, she tossed it into a pressure cooker along with carrots, onions, and seasonings. After setting the whole mess atop a burner, she headed for the other end of the downstairs.

Now that she knew what Liam was, she could research dragon shifters. The more she knew, the better she could protect herself. In case he hunted her down or something. Breath whistled from between her teeth. Crap on a cracker. What if she'd had sex with him, and he'd branded her somehow?

Worse, what if she actually wanted to walk away from her witchy heritage and follow him to wherever the dragons lived? Would fucking him turn her into a dragon shifter too? The idea repelled and excited her by turns. What would it be like to fly? To breathe fire?

To get laid a hundred feet in the air?

"Whoa, there, sweetie." Aisha put a lid on her thoughts. She was still desperate for the feel of a cock buried between her legs. Just thinking about it slicked her female bits with lust. She stopped in front of one of the home's many bookcases and drew a small box out from behind a magical tome. She'd be much more efficient researching Liam if she came first.

That way, her head wouldn't be fogged with lust and need and visions of his body naked and atop her, plumbing her with what was probably an amazing appendage. If his other form was a dragon, he had to be hung like no one's business.

She was breathing faster, and her heart hammered against her ribs as she pulled a dual stimulator from her treasure trove of sex toys. Women who had partners probably didn't need all those things. The variety and number of toys in the box spoke to how long she'd been alone. Any other day, she'd have felt sorry for herself, but she was too aroused to let her overflowing toy collection bring her down.

Her nipples had turned to distended peaks beneath her sweatshirt top. Reaching one hand beneath it, she cupped a breast and rolled the nipple between thumb and forefinger. Sensation rushed straight to her crotch, and she groaned, rubbing her thighs tight together.

The vibrator could wait for her second orgasm.

She inserted a hand beneath her waistband, shivering as her fingertips grazed her stomach before moving lower. Her clit was slick and swollen. She swirled an index finger around it before she abandoned any pretense of drawing this out and began to rub herself in earnest. Hard little circles that set her hips into a pagan rhythm as she thrust against her fingers.

Desire thickened the air around her until she could have sworn she tasted sex. Smelled it and was practically rolling in it. Her fingers snugged around her nipple and beat a tattoo against her clit. Far from elegant, orgasm caught her up and spun her around, leaving her breathless and shaking.

The shaking got her attention. She'd been so keyed up, she was still on her feet, hands thrust into her clothing like an errant teenager hoping to sneak in a climax with no one noticing.

The image made her laugh. She'd had plenty of surreptitious orgasms with a pillow stuffed between her legs, but not for a long time. Her nether regions still hummed with arousal. One climax had never been enough to satisfy her, but this time she sank to the floor and tugged one leg out of her sweatpants. She reached for her dual-headed vibrator with visions of Liam cavorting through her mind—a buck naked Liam with beautiful bronze skin and all his glorious hair tickling her as he strung kisses from the hollow in her neck to her breasts.

A lusty, *Mrowwww*, snapped her head up.

Hector sat about two feet away, leering at her.

Back when she'd thought he was a cat, she'd never given his presence a second thought, but now, when she was no longer certain, it felt perverse to frig herself in front of him.

"Shoo." She waved both hands in his direction.

Mrowwww. His pink tongue snaked out, sweeping across his upper lip, while his eerie feline gaze remained glued on her.

"So that's how it is, huh? Well, you have to go out and hunt sometime."

He shook his head twice, once to the left and once back to the right.

Fantasies of Liam aside, she was too self-conscious to continue, so she rolled onto one side and dropped the vibrator back into the box with all the other gadgets she'd collected.

"Fine." She wrinkled her nose at the cat and jumped to her feet. The pressure regulator was rocking like a dervish gone wild, so she turned down the heat beneath her stew and returned to the section of her library devoted to shifters.

Maybe not exactly "her" library, but it had fallen into her hands by default. Never mind all the generations of witches who'd gathered the books, scrolls, and tattered pages. Blowing off dust, she picked her way through the most promising shelf and tugged books and scrolls out as she went—along with a couple of leather-bound notebooks that looked like they dated back to the Middle Ages.

She poured herself a brandy and dragged her loot to a low table next to her favorite chair. Dinner would be at least an hour, even with the pressure cooker, and she'd make good use of the time. When she looked around for the cat, he was gone.

"Fucking voyeur," she called in the general direction of the cat door, but Hector didn't answer.

She hadn't expected him to.

Aisha was most of the way through dinner and her second brandy when she found what she'd been looking for. Focusing magic, she slogged through what turned out to be an early version of German mixed with Gaelic. After reading for an hour, she slumped against the creased-leather easy chair. The dragon shifters home world was Xara. They'd moved there a few centuries after Atlantis sank into the North Sea.

She'd always assumed Atlantis ended up in the Aegean, but she'd been wrong. Dragon shifters mated for life. Infidelity wasn't tolerated, nor were single dragons. Her mouth curved into a soft smile. What had Liam done to get himself kicked out of the fold. She'd bet her last spell it had something to do with sex. If any man lived, ate, and breathed sensuality, it was him.

What color was he as a dragon? How old? Dragon shifters weren't exactly immortal but close to it.

A puzzled whinny blasted through her mind, followed by a veritable cacophony. Aisha started to laugh. Her darlings wanted their dinner—and her. She always bid them good night and swathed them in protective magic. They were just like children, and they missed their nightly ritual.

She scrambled to her feet and walked her dish to the sink. The stew would keep overnight, so she pushed it to the back of the stove and settled the lid atop the pot. It had stopped raining at least an hour ago, but the yard would be muddy, so she shoved her feet into Muck boots and her arms into a rain slicker.

Flicking on the yard lights, she threaded her way among puddles and into the barn. The horses nickered and cooed, welcoming her. Aisha breathed deep. She loved horsey smells, and nothing compared with being surrounded by equine love. They adored her. She was their mother. Their goddess. It ran far deeper than her keeping the barn clean and their troughs full.

As she scratched ears and rubbed noses and passed out broken bits of carrot and apple she kept in a small fridge in the barn, she thought about Liam. He'd never fit into her life. The horses would sense his differentness and might react badly. They weren't overly fond of wolf shifters, viewing them the same way they saw wolves—as a potential enemy.

Dragons weren't exactly on their horsey radar, but she didn't expect things to go well. A brisk meow announced Hector's presence. The horses ignored him, and his only use for them was culling through discarded bits of food seeing if they'd left anything he might be interested in.

Hmmm. Not that Hector was anything like a dragon shifter, but she was pretty certain he wasn't a cat. If the horses accepted him, maybe she was wrong about Liam.

"Oh for pity's sake, get a life," she muttered.

The striking dragon shifter barely knew she existed, and here she was spinning fantasies about a life together. She was pathetic. Deserved her spinster status. She'd halfway been expecting him to pull into the driveway, but apparently her spell hadn't affected him the same way it might have influenced a lesser magic wielder.

She made a face. He must have felt the charm, known its source, and thumbed his nose at her efforts. Pretentious bastard. She'd always courted challenge with a bring-it-on vibe, but this was ridiculous.

If I'd known...

Her thoughts trailed off, remaining unfinished. Perhaps at some level, she had known, but she'd forged ahead anyway.

As if her visit gave them permission to pack it in for the night, the horses wandered into their stalls. She wove a protection spell, killed the lights, and slogged back to the house through puddles and mud. Maybe next summer she'd put in drainage tiles. She'd been planning to do that these past five years, but it was a huge job requiring a backhoe, which she'd have to rent.

Summers were busy. She always had newborn foals and customers stopping by to purchase either them—once they grew old enough to leave their mothers—or one of the older breeding stock. Resignation licked at her heels as she held the kitchen door open for Hector. Maybe this was the life that was ordained for her. It wasn't a bad one.

Once she got past the lonely part.

Hector strode past, tail still drooping from his stint outside in the rain. She shut the door, latching the cat door to keep raccoons and other small rodents out, and trudged up the ladder to her bed. A focused jot of magic lit one of her pillar candles. It sent crazy shadows creeping up the walls as she stripped out of her sweats and donned a flannel nightgown.

The garment had been her mother's, and if

anything made her feel like an old maid, it was this nightgown. Maybe that's why she'd selected it. To pound home that she'd never find a mate.

What had her grandmother said about the love charm? Oh yeah, that she should lie low for a couple days until it lost its punch. She could do that—for the most part. She'd made a commitment to help the other women set up a dance tomorrow night. Her part was decorations and serving booze-laden punch to the party-goers.

In truth, she'd been looking forward to the party. She almost never went anywhere. As it was, she'd have to explain to the horses they'd be going to bed without her tomorrow night. They wouldn't like it. They'd guilt-trip the hell out of her, which was why she rarely went anywhere.

Goddess's tits. What the hell was I thinking when I cast that love charm?

Only a horse-witch would put up with what I have to. Most people like to travel, go places. I can barely go out to dinner.

Before she sank deeper into a funk, she focused on the candleflame, letting it soothe her as she cast a relaxation spell. Her life hadn't changed one whit.

"Yeah, and that's the problem," she muttered. "Either I come to terms with that little fact, or I have to stand up to Mom and Grannie. Tell them to rustle up some other witch to watch over Lazy Witch Acres."

Her impromptu label brought a smile, but then she winced. Big words. Confronting her female kin would be a tough nut to crack. Easier to stuff her head up her ass like she'd been doing and let each day follow on the heels of the one before. She did love the horses. And they loved her.

She'd have to figure out a way to make sure their mutual admiration was enough.

CHAPTER 6

Earlier That Day

Liam had enjoyed a leisurely breakfast at The Rise and Grind, his favorite hole-in-the-wall coffee shop and café. He'd been deep in the New York Times when Jerry plopped down on the other side of the table and poured himself a coffee.

"Thanks, again, man." Jerry ladled enough sugar and cream into his mug to obliterate any benefit from the coffee. Inches shorter than Liam, he might have clocked in at five feet nine with a slight paunch. His fair hair was thinning, but he had a set of earnest blue eyes. Eyes that never changed, no matter how much of a line of bullshit Jerry was pumping out.

Liam laid the paper aside and glanced at his new breakfast mate. Jerry had clearly showered and changed. Still-damp brown hair had been carefully arranged over his bald spot, and circles ringed his blue eyes.

"No worries." Liam grinned. "All's well that ends well, eh?"

"Since when do you quote Shakespeare?" Jerry arched a brow.

"I do whatever fits, mate, and that line was perfect. You look beat. How come you're not home catching up on sleep?"

A middle-aged blonde waitress sidled close. "Breakfast, hon?" she asked Jerry. "After what you went through, it's on the house."

"Thanks, but I grabbed something at home."

"Well just holler if you change your mind." She trotted back through the swinging door into the kitchen.

"You never did answer me," Liam pressed.

"You mean why didn't I pitch face down on my bed and stay there?" At Liam's nod, he went on. "There's that dance tomorrow night. The women assigned a bunch of crap for me to do." He rolled his eyes. "You know how important these shindigs are to the gals. I had a bunch of spade work to roll out today, or I would have stayed home."

Liam culled through his memory and came up

with a vague recollection of a barn dance that had been rescheduled. Originally slated for Halloween Eve, something had happened that forced a change of plans. He refilled his cup from the pot sitting on the table and slugged back half of it. It wasn't all that hot anymore, but it was black and bitter, exactly the way he liked it.

"How come they moved it from Halloween again?" he asked.

"A bunch of the gals had conflicts with driving their kids to out-of-town football games. No one wanted to miss the fall dance, so they moved it to a better weekend." He leaned closer and lowered his voice. "Personally, I hate parties. Seems to give every single gal in town ideas."

Liam smirked. "Nothing wrong with that."

"No, not so long as they'd be satisfied with a roll in the hay, but every one I hook up with starts angling for a ring. They know I'm married, but that doesn't stop them."

"I get it." Liam made a clucking sound, hoping to convey male solidarity. He'd love to mine for every salacious detail. Apparently, Jerry slept around. Did his wife know? Even better, did she join in?

Since it wasn't any of his business, and he didn't really want a man-to-man conversation with any human, let alone Jerry, he grinned and said,

"Valentine's Day is right around the corner. Have you considered leaving town? Perhaps a trip to South America or Australia. At least its summer down under."

Jerry slapped a hand down on the table. "Why'd you have to go and remind me. V-Day is the absolute worst. Who the hell thought it was a good idea to create a holiday that revolved around Cupid?"

Liam had known Cupid personally, and he couldn't have agreed more, but that wasn't a tidbit he could drop on Jerry. Gathering the *New York Times*, he said, "I'll be shoving off. Didn't get any sleep last night, right along with you."

Jerry grinned. "I haven't forgotten. Hell, I'll never, never forget what you did for me. That check I promised should be on the floor of that little room you call an office." He narrowed his eyes. "Say, lots of decent business rentals in Stillwater. You've got some spare cash now, so maybe—?"

"No. Only reason I keep anything in town is so I'll have a place to meet clients."

Ever the real estate developer, Jerry kept right on talking. "But you could have a nicer place. One where you could justify raising your rates."

Liam stood. "The American way, eh? Bigger and better."

"Abso-fucking-lutely." Jerry stood and fist-bumped Liam. A cagey expression flitted across his features.

Aw crap. He wants something.

Liam raised an eyebrow. "I know that look. What now?"

"Go ahead, you can tell me," Jerry purred. "What'd they rope you into for tomorrow night's festivities?"

Liam took a step back. Of all the things to come out of Jerry's overactive mouth, he'd never have anticipated this one. "Er. Nothing."

The cagey expression edged farther into presumptuous territory. "Well, now. We can't have that. Misery loves company. You can help me set up for the band and get the food tables in order."

"Hold it right there, I'm scarcely a cook." Liam inhaled briskly. "You're better off tagging someone else. I'm happiest hanging off a rocky crag. Social events aren't exactly my forte."

"But, don't you see?" Jerry gripped Liam's upper arms "The women will go ape-shit over you since you don't come to dances."

"Which means they'll leave you alone. Hey, mate, take your hands off me."

Jerry's eyes pinched at the corners. Goddammit, he'd hurt the man's feelings. Liam hastily added, "I've got a piss pot of sore muscles from last night."

Jerry jumped back as if he'd been bitten. "Of course. Sorry. That was thoughtless of me." He angled his head, staring straight at Liam. "How about the dance? You could run home, clean up, take a few ibuprofen for those sore spots, and generally take it easy. If you met me back here around five tomorrow afternoon, I'd sure appreciate it."

Liam shuffled through excuses, but all of them sounded lame. Aisha probably wouldn't be there since she rarely left her stable of prime Arabians untended. She was the main one he wanted to avoid—at least until that senseless charm of hers ran its course.

Dancing was something that appealed to humans, although for the life of him, he'd never been able to figure out why. It wasn't much more than foreplay, so why not dive into the real thing and quit pretending it was anything else?

A corner of his mouth twitched downward. Jerry slugged him in the arm, and then said, "Whoops. Sorry. I'm sorry. Forgot how sore you are. How about tomorrow?"

He stopped shy of tacking a please onto the end of his sentence, but Liam picked up on his desperation. What the bloody fucking hell had the good ladies of Stillwater done to spook Jerry, beyond making a grab for his dick?

He opened his mouth to ask but shut it with a *clack*. He didn't really want all the nitty-gritty details.

Because it was the only way he was going to exit the café anytime soon, he said, "Fine. You wore me down. Five o'clock, where?"

The community building at the end of Main Street. We'll be using it and the barn. And no need to worry about cooking. The gals have that base covered. We'll mainly be doing the heavy lifting, moving the tables and chairs into formation. And the bandstand."

Liam slapped some money on the table and strode out of Rise and Grind with Jerry's thanks following him. His first stop was his office. As soon as he unlocked the door, a white envelope came into view. Liam scooped it up and looked inside. Sure enough, it contained a check for five grand made out to Liam with a note telling him to fill in his last name because Jerry wasn't sure how to spell it.

He folded the envelope and tucked it into a pocket before settling in at his desk. The office had a perpetually musty smell, so he left the door open. Going through his email and adding a few photos to social media didn't take long, but when he glanced at the clock in the corner of his screen, it was almost one in the afternoon.

Time to get moving. Not that he had anywhere particular to go but spending too much time boxed in with humans always made him feel antsy, uncomfortable, like he couldn't quite get a straight breath into him. Deep within, the dragon was restless. His ill-advised leap into pure, unbridled wantonness the other day had gotten the dragon going. It wanted to fuck too.

He'd gone over and over the fact there weren't any other dragons here, but his bondmate didn't care. It's parting shot had been something like, *"Then at least find a woman. We should not be reduced to servicing ourselves."*

While Liam privately agreed with him, women came with too many goddamned strings. He shut down his computer and got to his feet, pushing his desk chair back into its customary spot. Nothing more to do here, so he locked up and set off at a brisk pace.

He'd left the old Chevy beneath a grove of alder trees at the far end of town. He'd hidden it on purpose, in case that pesky witch showed up again, thinking to leave him a little gift—like a hex basket or a more potent love charm. It would be an easy-enough matter to sequester something like that in the rat's nest inside his car.

He really should clean it out. The floorboards were deep in fast food wrappers, obsolete climbing gear, and automotive tools. Whenever he needed something, it took forever to find it, which was why he kept his climbing gear *du jour* in the pickup bed. Liam cast subtle magic, hunting for Aisha. When her distinctive energy didn't ping back at him, he picked up his pace.

He balled one hand into a fist and slapped it into his other palm. Shit. He couldn't go the next few years avoiding her. If he knew anything about witches, they were tenacious little bitches. Even if the current spell frittered to nothing, the next one would have more oomph behind it.

He frowned. Did her horses have something to do with her magic? What would happen if he snuck up there one night and freed them? Would they leave? Or were they linked to her? Or to the land?

He blew out a frustrated breath. He had a lot of questions, and zero answers. The dragons had a phenomenal resource library that covered everything anyone would ever want to know about other varieties of magic-wielders, but it was on Xara. Not a location he could pop in and out of.

"Not a place I can return to at all without a mate," he muttered, bringing his other problem front and center.

Ten years was a long time, but if he didn't alter any of his patterns, he'd be just as mateless then as he was now. He reached the pickup, got in, and fired the engine, thinking about Aisha as he nosed the truck toward home. She might want him, but from the feel of the charm, it was only for sex.

A slow smile spread over his face. If he did invite her to his bed, she'd be so blown away by how great he was, she'd never want to leave. She already carried magic, so revealing what he was shouldn't give her a heart attack, like it might if she were human.

Yeah, but what then? Making love with him was a quantum world away from the ritual that would turn her into a dragon shifter so both of them could return to Xara. He gripped the wheel harder. This was the same problem he always ran up against. A woman might be taken with him, but no woman was ever taken enough to do anything beyond blanch when he floated the idea of leaving Earth behind.

The few who'd stayed around long enough for him to get that far had developed that special look in their eyes mothers reserve for the mentally deficient—or the mad. He'd had to wipe their memories of everything about him because he couldn't risk one of them telling anyone what he truly was.

Humans would think he had a few screws loose, but other magic wielders would know the truth, and they'd hound him until they discovered the location of his hoard. They'd end up in a pitched battle, and it wouldn't be pretty. Part of the covenant among their kind stated no unnecessary killing—unless a hoard was threatened.

Except for vampires, of course. They were always fair game.

Whether a supernatural judge would view protecting his hoard as justification for murder remained to be seen. Maybe if the judge was another dragon shifter, but probably not if they were something else.

He turned down the long, rutted lane leading to his mining cabin, his mind full. He'd just gotten out of the car, determined to clean up the cab's interior, when a jolt of sexual energy blasted him in the groin. It had Aisha's feel all over it.

He snorted, blowing smoke and fire out of his mouth. He'd been right about one thing: she wasn't about to give up. Desire curled around the base of his spine and gripped him, sending tendrils lower. His cock shot to attention. Hot, distended, throbbing with need.

He ground his teeth and splayed his hands over the truck hood. "I will not do this," he said, repeating the words. His cock jerked where it curved against his belly, hard as it ever got. Ignoring the siren call of sex, the urgency to drive himself hard and fast into a woman, he walked to the passenger side and dragged the door open.

The slimy, sneaky bitch had found his truck after all. She'd hidden a charm somewhere in the heaps of trash, but he'd find it, and when he did, she'd be in for a hell of a surprise. All he needed was something of hers, and he could cast a little mischief of his own.

Liam dragged handfuls of everything from paper to crescent wrenches out of his truck, chucking everything in a pile on the ground. He'd sort things later. For now, he had to locate the offending bit of witchcraft. When he crouched to reach behind the seat back, it stretched his pants across his erection. He was panting, arousal spilling through him.

He had almost everything out from behind the seat but for a set of ascenders. He'd been missing them for months. Damn. His house might be neat, but he ran a sloppy ship in some ways. When he angled his body half into the space behind the seat, his cock slithered up and down against the doorframe.

Liam realized what he'd done, but it was too late. Semen juddered from him as he lay half in and half out of the truck. It took the edge off his arousal, but he was totally disgusted with himself. He hadn't come in his pants since he was a gawky adolescent, fielding perpetual erections that never truly went away.

Sucking air like a bellows, he backed away from his truck. At least he had everything out of it. A dollop of semen slithered down one leg. He drove a fist into a nearby tree and hurried into the house to change. He could pick up the mess in the driveway once he didn't stink of sweat and lust. Worry nagged. Had his orgasm given her something to latch onto? A way to inveigle her way into his mind and torment him until he broke down and fucked her?

He'd gone to a lot of trouble to sequester himself behind a magic barrier before bringing himself off a couple of days back. This climax caught him bare-assed. Not much he could do about it, though, since it had already happened.

It was only much later—after he'd cleaned up and changed—he realized he hadn't found Aisha's love charm. Hadn't found anything that shouldn't be in his truck except a mouse nest. He shook his head as he straightened the rest of the debris that had been cluttering his truck cab. She must command some hella powerful magic to have this effect on him without a physical object to anchor her spell.

His stomach rumbled, and he went back inside and set about grabbing items from the fridge. He draped a raw steak across a frying pan, cooking it just long enough to remove the chill. Next came a box of scalloped potatoes. He tossed everything into a bowl, added milk and butter, and nuked it. He could have accomplished much the same effect breathing on it, but this was faster.

The loaf of bread was hard as a rock, so he cut slices and wrapped them in a damp towel to rehydrate.

They'd be good to go once his steak and potatoes were done. He dropped into a nearby chair and tried to come up with an excuse for welching on Jerry tomorrow night.

Last thing he felt like doing was socializing, particularly if Aisha could commandeer his libido from miles away and turn him into a pile of sex-driven mush. He still didn't understand how she'd made him come, and the lack of control freaked him worse than anything he'd run into since Grigori exiled him from Xara.

He'd just snatched his steak off the stove and checked on the potatoes—they weren't quite done, but he'd eat them the way they were rather than waiting—when his phone blatted its ringtone.

Loud and obnoxious, the trumpeting elephant guaranteed he'd always hear the device. After a longing glance at his meal, he snatched up the phone and tapped *Accept.* "Liam here."

Last call he'd taken, he'd ended up on that SAR mission. No matter what whoever was calling wanted, he was going to eat his dinner first.

"Of course, it's you," a deep, female voice crooned.

Liam sat straighter. He knew that voice but couldn't quite place it. "I'm afraid you have me at a disadvantage—" he began.

"Just the way I like it," the woman went on. "I'm Victoria Colewright, and we need to talk."

Understanding crashed over him until he wanted to retreat to his cave and curl up on his hoard. "Aye, I recall who you are," he stammered.

"Damn good thing."

Before she could say anything more, he blurted, "You're Aisha's kinswoman."

"Brilliant deduction. Are you going to blither on all night, or are you ready to listen?"

He bristled. No one talked to him like that. Not even a witch he'd lusted over eighty years ago. He'd been newly arrived on Earth and bolder, but she'd never taken him up on his seduction schemes.

A long-drawn sigh rattled through the cellular line. "Don't get your scales ruffled, dragon. This won't take long, and then you can tuck into that man-food you're calling dinner. Tsk. Tsk. Not a vegetable in sight."

He jumped to his feet, scattering magic in a circle. Where the fuck was she? She had to be close if she knew what he was about to eat. Nothing witchy was anywhere nearby, though. The evidence of how powerful she was brought him up short. No one should have magic like that—other than dragon shifters.

"Ready to listen?" She was almost purring.

"Yes." He ground out the word.

"Good." The purr was gone, replaced by a tone

sharp as any razor. "My granddaughter was stupid. Do not react to her spell. When she cast it, she had no idea what you are, but she knows now. Are we quite clear about that?"

"Yeah. I guess so. Why's it so important to you? If you're the grandmother who used to live on the horse ranch, you're supposed to be dead."

"Oh please. I thought even you were smarter than that. Stay away from Aisha."

Liam was recovering fast. "And if I don't?" he countered, still nonplussed at being dressed-down by a not-exactly-dead witch.

"You don't want to test me, young man. I'm as tough an adversary as you're likely to meet. Besides, you've been gone from Xara so long, you've grown soft."

"Why you self-righteous old bat." He shook a fist at the air.

"Now, now. Stick and stones, youngster. Sticks and stones."

Witch presence vanished as quickly as it had shown up. Too keyed up to eat, he stared at his cooling food.

"*Eat!*" his dragon roared to the accompaniment of smoke and flames.

"Fuck all of you," Liam snarled and stormed out into the yard. He was no one's patsy. No one's. Not

Aisha's. Not Victoria's. And certainly not his bondmate's.

He'd eat when he was good and ready, and not a moment sooner. And he might not stay out of Aisha's path, either. Maybe she was exactly the mate he'd been hunting all these years. Handy she knew he was a dragon shifter. It would save a whole lot of explanations.

 isha glanced at her phone—again. It was twenty to nine, and she'd been serving punch to an increasingly inebriated crowd for almost three hours. The night was cold and clear, the sky shot with millions of stars. She breathed deep, loving the pine and sage smells along the lower reaches of the Sierras. Small rodents chittered from thick forest across the way, and the cries of nighthawks and owls on the hunt added to the rest of the evening's music.

The band wasn't bad, sort of a combination of bluegrass and country. She'd found herself swaying to its beat more than once as the hours wore on. Things had been going well until she caught a flash of Liam's rangy form a while back.

Panic mingled with leftover lust. In an attempt to avoid him—maybe not him, precisely, but all the complications around pursuing him—she'd shrouded herself in invisibility. She was still concealed when someone wanting more punch had simply helped themselves. Once they staggered back into the crowd, she released her spell.

"Sure you don't want a break?" Arabia Jenson sidled close on clunky heels designed to mask her short, chunky stature. Her black hair was streaked with turquoise, and she was duded up as usual with way too much makeup and jewelry for Aisha's taste. Despite the chill evening, Arabia wore a flimsy top, and a tight corset that pushed most of her breasts into view.

Aisha swallowed distaste. She'd never had much use for overdone women, and if anyone took it to the max, it was Arabia. "Nah, I'm good. Lucy May said she'd take over at nine."

Arabia quirked a brow. "Cool. Then you can party all you want."

Aisha choked on a snort. "Nope. No parties for this gal. I'll be heading home. I hate leaving the horses alone for very long."

"Don't you think you're a wee bit overprotective?"

"No. I don't." She resisted the urge to tell Arabia to get lost, but Stillwater was too small to make enemies.

"Aw, come on." Arabia grinned engagingly. "Have a little fun for once. I'm sure your horsies are all bedded down for the night."

A hot tide of words wanted out; Aisha stifled a desire to blast the bitch smiling at her. She'd never liked the woman who ran a phony psychic shop out of her home. Further, she'd always resented the similarities between Arabia's name and her beloved Arabian stable.

Arabia had magic of some sort, but Aisha had never cared enough to tease out what kind.

Offering a tight smile, she said, "Nope. Heading home."

"Fine. Have it your way." Arabia lowered her voice and leaned close. "I have a surprise planned for around nine, but you'll still be here for it."

Aisha didn't like the sound of *surprise* coming from a neophyte who dabbled in magical places she didn't belong, but before she could mine for details, Arabia sauntered away, hips swinging. Not quite lost in the crowd, she latched onto that lawyer boyfriend of hers.

Aisha ground her teeth and wished she'd put more effort into figuring out exactly what kind of magic Arabia had. Was the woman as green as she suspected? Or did she command enough power to make a true botch of whatever this *surprise* turned out to be?

Where the hell was Lucy? If she showed up soon, Aisha would make a run for it. That way, she'd escape whatever "harmless fun" Arabia was cooking up with her crystals and wands and whatever other props she employed.

Aisha closed her teeth over her lower lip. She liked things nice, clean, simple. It was how she orchestrated her magic—and her life. She'd bet her ranch Arabia's spells were as overstated as she was with unnecessary—and unpredictable—embellishments tacked on because they were shiny.

Another peek at her phone told her that her stint would be up in ten more minutes. *Come on, Lucy,* she urged silently.

"Hey, honey! Did this turn into self-serve?" A fair-haired man she didn't recognize planted the flats of his hands on the punch table, leering at her through greenish eyes.

Not caring for his tone, she ladled punch into a paper cup and set it in front of him. "Here you go."

"I had another type of self-serve in mind." He ogled her breasts.

"Get lost."

"Now, that is no way to treat a guest."

Never her long suit, Aisha's temper snapped, and she stomped around to his side of the long table. "It is if the guest in question is an ill-tempered boor."

His eyes widened in shock. From the looks of his polished boots and fancy clothes, he was some rich dude used to people fawning all over him. "I'll report you to—to someone. See you lose your job."

"Nothing would make me happier. Go away."

"I love it when you wenches play hard to get." He surged forward, making a grab for her breasts, but she was far faster than him, and she pivoted sideways. He stumbled, almost falling. Before he could turn around for another go at her, she hurried back to her side of the table. Straightening, he glared at her, snapped up his punch, and stomped away.

Nine o'clock.

Where the fuck was Lucy? Had she forgotten her promise to take over as punch-maid? Aisha had just decided to hunt her down, with magic if need be, when the singsong cadence of a spell reached her sensitive hearing.

"Pray, *hear my words, Ceridwen,*
   Mother of Magic,
   Goddess who is Wise.
   Upon this full moon dark, this season of ice,
   When the mists between the worlds are thin,
   I call upon your power to arise and come to me.
   Heart's desire called forth.
   Ceridwen, assess my worth.

Freedom from slavery, naked in your rites.

Liberated from fear and doubt this night.

Before the dawn, deliver my heart's delight and desire.

Love is the law unto all beings.

My will be done, so mote it be."

AISHA'S MOUTH rounded into a horrified moue. This was Arabia's surprise? It sure as hell was her chanting the Heart's Desire spell. Layered atop the spell Aisha had put into play to snare Liam, the two were bound to be additive. Her muscles hardened into blocks of apprehension. She waited through one breath, and then another.

Nothing happened.

Maybe this would be all right. Perhaps Ceridwen was off-duty, looking elsewhere, or simply not paying one whit of attention to such a minor player in the magical cast of characters.

Wishful thinking. Just because Aisha hoped for all those things was absolutely zero guarantee any of them were true.

"I've got to get out of here," she muttered. "Right now. People are drunk enough, and they can get their own damned punch."

She grabbed her bag and set off for where she'd left her truck a few blocks away, but her body wouldn't cooperate. She thought she was leaving, but she ended up walking in circles, driven by magic as strong as she'd ever experienced. All around her, couples were falling into each other's arms. The sound of kisses and moans rose, accompanied by the reek of lust gone wild.

So much for Ceridwen looking elsewhere.

Her own body hummed with desire. All her fantasies about Liam crowded into her mind creating a Bacchanalian collage of one lust-ridden scene after another. She realized she'd stopped moving midway between a food site and her abandoned punch table.

The smell of smoke drew her at a run, and she turned off the food venue's untended hot plates. They'd been making some kind of stir-fry, and the oil had begun to smoke. Thank the goddess, she'd noticed it before it went up like a torch. Grease fires were the absolute worst.

Every movement turned into an erotic ballet. Her shirt brushing her erect nipples drove her mad. Her jeans hiked into her crotch, and she almost came from the pressure. She had to get out of here, but she couldn't remember where her truck was.

Or anything else.

The couples around her had moved from kissing to pawing at one another. When she glanced up, she saw a woman on her knees with a man's dick moving in and out of her mouth. Aisha couldn't stand it. She shoved a hand between her legs. Maybe if she came, she'd remember where her truck was.

Ha. Not likely. If this is the casting I think it is, it will last for hours, maybe days. Shit. Crap. Fuck. How did that flamboyant bitch have the skill to pull it off?

She thrust her hips hard against the hand cupped around her vulva. Not long. This would happen soon, very soon. She shut her eyes, calling up her favorite image of Liam, copper hair blowing in the wind, green eyes crinkled at their corners, chiseled lips grinning.

"Now, that's what we like, lass." His brogue was so real, she was certain her fantasy had come to life.

Arms closed around her from behind, and the unmistakable bulge of an erection prodded her backside. He placed his hand on top of the one she had between her legs, displacing hers. Heat from his hand seared her. The scents of clay baked under a Mediterranean sun mingled with rosemary and grew around them.

Aisha gasped, and her eyes flew open. "Oberon's balls! You're real. It's not just in my head."

"Aye, lass. I'm real enough. There's strong magic afoot—and not yours this time. I say we go with it."

She never knew where she got the strength to slither out from beneath his erotically-charged touch and swing around to face him. Sure enough, the clean lines of his face hovered above her. High forehead, square jaw, and those lips that all but begged her to kiss them.

"I was trying to leave."

"The spell wouldn't let you." He swung one arm wide, encompassing dozens of rutting, half-naked couples. No one seemed to care it was too cold for that much exposed flesh.

She took a deep breath. It wasn't easy. What she wanted to do was join the fuck-fest on the lawn. "Is that why you're here?"

His green eyes turned into twin flames that drew her. "Nay, lassie. 'Tis strong enough magic, but mine trumps everything."

"If that's true"—another ragged breath—"why are you still here?"

He cupped the side of her face in his big, calloused fingers. "Because you are. Couldn't leave you to the antics of just any Lothario with a hard-on, now could I?"

The corners of her mouth twitched. "You did sense my love charm. Admit it."

He tossed his head, nostrils flaring. "Aye, a man would have to be dead not to feel such a calling." He moved the hand cradling her face and hooked an index finger beneath her chin. "Where I come from, men prefer to pick their bedmates without artificial inducements."

"But I waited and waited. I flirted. I—" She clapped a hand over her mouth. Whatever was wrong with her? She should shut up. "Never mind," she mumbled.

"You don't understand." He grasped one of her hands and pressed it over his erection.

Heat roared through her. Contact with the hot, thick, throbbing length almost brought her to her knees. She grappled with the buttons on his jeans, but he tugged her hands away.

"We are going to do this," he said, his voice rough with need, "but not out here on the ground like rutting beasts." Sweeping an arm downward, he caught the backs of her knees and swung her into his arms.

She pushed her shoulder bag aside, so it wasn't jammed between their bodies and twined her arms around his neck. They shouldn't do this, but she didn't see any other way out of the sexual tide that had sucked her into its maw. All the hand jobs in the world wouldn't slake her lust.

Liam buried his nose in her hair before stringing kisses down the side of her face. He carried her as if she weighed nothing, taking them away from the grunts and groans as people orgasmed right and left around them. Angling her head to meet his questing mouth, she kissed him, drinking him deep.

He tasted the way she thought gold might taste, bright and metallic with sweet undertones. She should find out where he was taking her, but she didn't care so long as they could get naked. He snaked his tongue into her mouth; she sparred with it and then tongue-kissed him back.

Nibbles, bites, and more kisses ignited need so pervasive it drove everything but the man next to her to a distant planet. Nothing had ever existed beyond this moment. Nothing ever would.

He ripped his mouth from hers. "My office is the closest place. It's not fancy, but—"

"Close is good." She could barely get the words out. The prospect of the fifteen-minute drive to her house or however far his was felt untenable. Unthinkable.

Magic glowed hot around them as he entered her mind. A lazy grin full of promise spread over his face. "Brilliant. I want you to be just as hungry as I am, and be warned, no one is as hungry as a mating dragon."

Dragon.

Dragon.

Dragon.

The word sent warning bells pealing through her

head, and she wriggled in his grasp. "We can't. I mean I want to, but we can't. It's a bad idea. I—"

The magic swirling through her mind developed a soothing aspect, rather akin to the energy she used to calm restless horses. He held her closer and whispered to her in Gaelic.

She tried to find more words, but they twisted into arcane runes before spooling out of existence. The energy from the Heart's Desire spell throbbed around them. His erection prodded her side, and she remembered how it felt in her hand. The need to strip him bare and study every inch before devouring him raced through her, heady like fragrant brandy.

"Better," he crooned in Gaelic. "We must do this, Aisha. Between your spell and the ill-conceived one blanketing Stillwater, we've no choice."

"You could have picked someone else."

"In all the years I've been here, I've kept to myself. You're who I want, lass, who I long for. You're in my mind when I stroke myself. What do you know about the Heart's Desire spell?"

The question caught her off-guard. "Not much, other than I recognize it." She glanced away, suddenly shy. "I don't expect you'll believe me, but I don't normally employ magic to lure men to my bed."

"I hear truth in your words." He nodded and kissed her forehead. "We're almost to my office. The

Heart's Desire spell is a love spell wound in with a truth spell. It flogs whoever hears it with an insatiable lust, but only for their one true love. It's why almost no one was coupling with their husbands or wives back there." He jerked his head the direction they'd come.

She met his direct, green-eyed gaze. "So your story about saving me from an errant Lothario was bullshit."

He snorted laughter. "Not entirely. 'Tis possible you had a suitor I knew naught about, but I wasn't taking any chances."

She tightened her hold on his neck, loving how it pressed her breasts into his chest. "What if the attraction is one-sided?"

"Then Heart's Desire only pushes half the equation." The lazy, liquid-sex grin returned. "One-sided isn't a problem between us, lass. You want me as hard as I want you."

She didn't bother to deny it.

He stopped in front of a nondescript door and set her on her feet. Power flashed from his upraised hand, and the door flew open. He mimed a low, sweeping bow. "After you, Madam Witch."

A shock ran through her. No one addressed her magic so directly, and she cast a furtive glance around to make sure no one had been within hearing range.

He shrugged. "You know what I am. I know what

you are. Saves a lot of time—and explanations. Time we could be otherwise engaged."

Aisha moved beneath the lintel. The feel of dragon shifter magic surrounded her, almost stifling in its intensity. She wanted to breathe it in, let it mingle with her power. The click of a door shutting sounded behind her.

Liam beckoned with a crooked finger and led the way through into a smaller room. Opening a closet, he pulled sleeping bags out of it and arranged them into a beckoning nest on the floor. Light glowed from power spilling through him. Breath hitched in her throat until it was tough to swallow.

She'd never wanted anyone as much as she wanted the dragon.

Lithe as a big jungle cat, he moved in front of her and unzipped her coat, dropping it on top of the piled sleeping bags. Running his hands from her shoulders to her waist, he hooked his fingers underneath her top and yanked it over her head, leaving her in her long underwear. Aisha didn't need to glance down to know her nipples stood in stiff peaks, tenting the fabric of the last bit between her and her upper torso being naked.

"Christ, wench, how many layers of clothes do you need? 'Tis like being back in the Middle Ages where women wore so much, I never bothered to undress them. Took too long."

Feeling bold, she dragged the silken long-sleeved top off and tossed her shoulders back, looking straight at him.

He made a uniquely male sound with overtones of bugling dragon before he dove at her, burying his face in her breasts. She shrieked at the feel of his mouth on her distended nipples. The need to feel all of him against her was overpowering as she tumbled them onto the cushy pile of down sleeping bags.

CHAPTER 8

If Liam thought he was lost before, the sight of the high, mounded globes of Aisha's breasts undid him. He couldn't have held himself back any more than he could have held back the tides, and he latched onto a coppery nipple with his mouth. By Pan and all the lusty gods, the witch in his arms was made for sex. For loving.

For me, a voice growled deep within. *She was made for me.*

Aye, she's mine. Dragon possessiveness blasted to the forefront of his mind.

Aisha grappled with his ancient denim, fleece-lined jacket while arching into his hungry kisses as he moved from one breast to the other. Reaching back, he tugged on a sleeve until the coat slithered aside. She started unbuttoning his shirt, but after the first button got caught in an errant thread, she gripped the cotton and ripped it open.

Liam let go of her breasts long enough to tip his head back and laugh. "Go for it, wench. You can destroy as many of my clothes as you want."

She was breathing hard, and lively rose splotches covered her chest and face. "Naked," she panted and reached for the buttons to his jeans. "We need to be naked. Now."

"Aye, naked would make this so much easier." He undid his belt. By then, she had his jeans open and was working her fingers inside. "Hang on, sweetheart." He hated to turn away from those wonderful breasts, but he had to lever his boots off. The bootjack was in the other room, so he worked the toe of one boot against the heel of the other until it gave way. He dragged the other boot off with both hands.

"Oh yeah. Boots," she mumbled and went to work on hers. "What the fuck did cowboys do?"

"Women wore skirts in those days." Boots out of the way, he pushed his jeans down his legs and grinned rakishly. Damn, she made him hot, but in a way that felt like he'd come home.

She snickered. "Skirts as in just huck 'em up and go for it?"

"That was precisely how it worked, a great improvement from the Middle Ages I might add." He unfastened her Levi's and got hold of them, peeling the skin-tight denim down her legs.

"And you'd know those things how?" She arched a brow and wriggled beneath his touch before making a grab for the tented-out front of his shorts.

"How else, lass? I was there. We live a long time, as do you." He tossed her pants aside. All that stood between him and seeing all of her was a lacy, black thong. He tapped the elastic that rode low on her hips. "Pretty fancy. Were you planning on a gentleman caller?"

"Can't a girl have nice things just for herself?" she countered and wrapped a hand around his unruly appendage. "Wow. Just wow. Why'd you leave the shorts on? I want to see all of you."

Before Liam could divest himself of his jockeys, she'd done it for him, dragging the bit of white cotton down his legs. He slithered the rest of the way out of them, intensely aware of her gaze glued to him. He met the heat of her hazel eyes, glittering orbs that shone violet in the light bleeding from his magic. "Do I pass inspection?"

Instead of answering, she launched herself at him, twining her arms around his neck as her mouth crashed over his. The skin-to-skin contact made his head spin. Deep inside, his dragon bugled an unmistakable mating call. Aisha might not be a dragon shifter, but his dragon wanted her for their mate.

It should have scared the bejesus out of him, sent him running for the hills, but he kissed her harder. Biting, sucking, licking over the sting from the bites with more kisses. Where they pressed into his chest, her nipples were hard as polished agates. He ached to suckle them again.

Hell, he wanted to do everything all at once. Lick her. Suck her. Kiss her. Fuck her. Just gazing at her perfectly proportioned body would have been enough —for a while, anyway. Her slender waist flared to generous hips, and she had an ass a man could die for. Muscles bunched the length of her legs from all her time on horseback.

She could ride me.

The thought of dipping and swooping through the air with her thighs spread across his scaled back thrilled him and upped the ante on his lust.

She was making little moaning noises as she drove her hips into him where she'd straddled one thigh. The heat from her core seared him, and her scent—new-mown, sweet hay mingled with musky undertones—rose around them. He inhaled hungrily, wanting to absorb every molecule.

He explored her mouth with his tongue, delighted when she sparred with him and plumbed his mouth.

She tasted sweet, like the whiskey punch from earlier in the evening. He ran his fingertips down her back, learning her body as he went. His plan was to cup her generous ass and roll her over, but before he could do that, she broke their kiss and slithered down his body, mouth trailing heat as she went. When she detoured to his nipples, pinching them, it took everything he had not to come.

His mind was foggy from lust, his body on fire with desire so pervasive it took over, trumping everything. She'd continued her lazy traverse of his body with her teeth and tongue. When she took the head of his cock in her mouth, he cried out. A hot, primitive, feral shriek that shocked him. Even when he'd mated as a dragon, he'd never sounded like that.

She gripped his shaft with both hands and ran her mouth up and down him. Everywhere she touched ignited and blazed hot. He jackknifed his body until her female bits were in reach of his tongue. Reaching around, he grabbed the ass he'd been lusting after and fastened his mouth over her distended nub.

Her mouth tightened around him, and she sucked harder, alternating sucking with nipping around the sensitive head. He groaned and pushed into her mouth. Sex developed a life of its own. He wanted to be inside her, but that could wait for their next round.

Her clit shivered beneath his tongue, and he moved

one hand to push two fingers inside her. Damn but she was hot and ready. He worked her between his mouth and his hand, thrilled when her vault dissolved around him into the rhythmic contractions of an orgasm. Liam lost himself in her ecstasy, and his own control slipped away.

Maybe she was using magic, but she knew how close he was and rubbed him harder, faster. When she dipped a finger into his ass, he came. Great shuddering spasms ripped from his belly, twisted him around, and wrung him out. She kept right on stimulating him until the last jolts faded. Even then, she didn't let go.

Very reluctantly, he extricated himself from of her mouth, flipped back around, and covered her mouth with his. She tasted of him, and his cock, which hadn't subsided much, was instantly erect again. Drawing back, he grinned at her. Damn, he hadn't ever felt this randy. He could fuck this woman forever and still want more. He broke their kiss, wanting to tell her she was almost his, but words eluded him.

"I know that look." She eyed him coquettishly.

"You do, eh?"

"Aye." She aped his brogue.

"Excellent. Then you understand we're far from done with one another. I'm going to impale you, fuck you until you shatter. How do you want us to be?"

She grinned back. "Love the imagery. It's raw—and erotic."

"How do you want us to be?" he repeated, driven by urgency to thrust deep into her and never leave.

"Giving the lady a choice, huh?"

"Only if you decide in the next five seconds." He wrapped a hand around his hard-on and rubbed it against her belly.

"How about this?" She slithered out from under him and turned over, rising onto her hands and knees. Her amazing, stellar ass parted displaying her sex with its frame of golden curls to perfection.

For long moments, he just gazed at her, unbelieving. She was flawless, a goddess. He could stare at that vista forever and—

She twisted her head until she could see him. "Well? You don't like it this way?"

"I adore it. I was admiring the view. You have the finest ass in all the world, lassie." With a determined growl, he surged forward planting himself at the opening to her body.

After gifting him with a smile worthy of Aphrodite, she hip-butted him, the invitation obvious. He sank into her slowly, giving her time to stretch around his girth. She wanted him to move, to fuck her hard and fast. The erratic motions from her spelled that out loud and clear, but he'd come once, which meant he could stretch this out, make it last until both of them cried for mercy. For release.

He twined his magic with hers once he was fully encased in the heat of her body, and began a long, slow dance where he withdrew and pushed back inside. Sometimes he moved a wee bit faster, until she hovered on the edge of release, but then he backed off.

She panted, ground her hips, cried out, and cursed him, but he retained control. He was panting too, caught up in his own game. She kept trying to frig herself. After the dozenth time he'd batted her hands away from her swollen nub, he pulled out of her and turned her onto her back.

"Goddammit!" She wound her legs around his waist, pulling until he sank back inside her.

Liam captured her wrists, holding her arms above her head with one hand as he settled into the rhythm she wanted. Top to bottom as fast as he could move. It was time. For both of them. They were so primed from his teasing, bringing them to the brink and then stopping, she didn't last a dozen strokes before her body quivered around his exquisitely sensitive hard-on.

Liam released the brakes. The climax that had been simmering just below a boiling point blasted out of him. Somewhere between spasms, he bent his head and bit her shoulder.

Or rather, his dragon did.

She was so far sunk in lust, the bite pushed her into another orgasm that seeded itself from the aftershocks of the one she'd just had. He kept on coming too, pumping semen into her until he had no idea what would happen next.

Would they come forever, locked in one another's arms?

It was an enthralling idea, but their bodies finally quieted after grinding and straining against each other. He rolled them onto their sides, loving the feel of her skin and her curves. He had to tell her what he'd done but didn't know how.

Those conversations—the ones about mating bites and what they meant—were supposed to happen before the event, not after.

She smoothed long strands of sweaty hair back from his face. "This wasn't just the Heart's Desire spell, was it?"

The question was as good an entry point as he was likely to get. He cradled the side of her face in his hand. "Nay, sweetheart. Your love charm coupled with Heart's Desire may have added a wee bit of extra spice, but what just happened was you and me."

Her mouth, soft and gentle in the aftermath of lovemaking, turned up at one corner. "This has been amazing. So incredible I don't have words for how fantastic you were, but I have to get home. The horses will be in a terrible snit. It might take bags of carrots and apples before they deign to forgive me."

"But..." he sputtered. He had to tell her, and he'd been off to a decent start.

"But what?" She arched both brows into twin question marks.

"There are things we must talk about. For that, we need time."

She frowned, forming a small vertical furrow in her forehead. "I suppose you could come home with me, but Grannie may show up, and she'll figure out soon enough what happened. She won't be pleased."

"Aye, I know that all too well. Victoria paid me a visit."

Aisha drew back. "She did?" At his nod, her beauty developed harsh edges. "Why that meddling old bat."

"She cares about you. 'Tisn't necessarily a bad thing." Liam was sidestepping the major issue, which was they were now mated through this life and every one that would come after, but he had no idea how Aisha would react. Never mind the becoming a dragon shifter so she could return to Xara with him part. She had a temper, which meant she might blow up, and he couldn't stand the possibility of her being angry with him. Even if he deserved it.

Man up, for god's sake.

The edges of her magic probed his mind. He slammed the door on her explorations fast.

She drew away from him and sat up. "What is it? You're hiding something from me. Do you have wives stashed in every port?"

Her guess was so far off the mark, he laughed.

"Don't dismiss me," she bridled and began dragging on her discarded clothing.

He knelt in front of her and placed his hands on her shoulders. "Nay. No wives. That's not it. I owe you a long talk, but now's not the time. May I follow you home?"

She closed her teeth over her lower lip. At least she quit tossing on clothes. "The horses. They might not like you, and they'll be pissed off enough at me for deserting them."

"You never leave them alone?"

"Not for more than a couple of hours." She shrugged, looking uncomfortable and defensive. "My magic is woven in with the land that ranch sits on. It includes the horses, so they're bound to me. They're not like normal horses. If I'm not there, they sense something is missing, and they're smart enough to know it's me." She paused to take a measured breath. "Their little horsey worlds don't feel right if a Colewright witch isn't front and center."

"What happens when enough time passes, you

have to leave so the townspeople don't catch on there's something odd about you. They're getting older, and you're not."

"Why do you think I cast that love charm?" she shot back. "I have to get rolling producing my replacement. It's not going to happen all by itself." Aisha rubbed at the place he'd bitten her in the junction between neck and collarbone. She was savvy enough, she might figure things out quick enough even absent explanations from him. He couldn't allow that to happen.

"I really would like to follow you. If my presence bothers the horses, I'll leave. Promise."

"As soon as I say, with no arguments?" She nailed him with her direct gaze.

"Aye." He made an X across his chest. "Cross my heart."

She laughed. "Haven't heard that one since I was a girl. All right, Liam Fiontan. It's a deal." She extended a hand, and he shook it.

Liam gathered his underwear and jeans, getting back into them. By the time he was working his feet into socks and boots, Aisha was dressed and ready to leave.

"My truck's not far from here," she said. "Do you know where my ranch is?"

It was a reasonable question, but he hedged,

substituting flattery for truth as he said, "I'm a dragon. I can find anything. Particularly treasure like you." He stopped shy of telling her that now they were mated, he'd be able to find her no matter where she was. On this world or any other.

His dragon bugled annoyance. *"Coward!"* It threw the word in his face, and he cringed.

Worry creased the corners of her eyes into pinwheels. "Is something wrong? Is Grannie nattering away in the wings?"

Her concern smote him. He wanted her to care about him, but he had to tell her the truth. He'd take care of that as soon as they were at her ranch. If he cloaked his power, the horses wouldn't react badly. "Everything's fine. I'll see you in a little bit."

He wrapped his arms around her and gave her a quick, intense kiss before she walked through his office and out into the night. Her scent was thick in his nostrils, and it was a struggle not to follow her.

Retreating to straighten his office, he got his other boot on and then headed for his pickup. It wasn't much past midnight, and the thrum of the Heart's Desire spell still permeated the air. It wouldn't fade for a few hours yet. He rolled his shoulders back. Who the hell had thought it was a good idea to cast such a potent version of that particular spell? Larger cities had at least a skeleton supernatural-law-enforcement presence, but Stillwater was far too rural.

Still, he hoped the miscreant spell-caster would be held to answer for what they'd done. While he was familiar with the casting, he'd never felt quite this powerful a version of it.

He reached his truck and got in, firing the engine.

"When are you going to tell her?" The dragon was back, or more likely it had never left.

"Soon."

"Before she discovers she can't get us out of her mind and thinks she's gone mad?" the dragon countered smugly. *"She bears my mating bite. There's no way out of that. She's ours. Forever."*

"You think I don't know all that? It would have been bad enough just making love, but she'd still have had an out. Before you bit her."

"Aye, clever of me."

"I can think of other words, like sneaky and underhanded." Steam puffed from Liam's mouth. He opened the window fast before the inevitable flames followed. "I suppose next you'll demand to fly."

"Nay. Next, we must tell the lass she's bound to us forever. And then, we shall petition the dragons' council on Xara to allow us to return early. Since we're mated, I'm certain they'll—"

"Hold up, *bondmate*." Liam stressed the last word. "You bit her because you want to go home."

He waited. The dragon didn't deny it, so he forged ahead. "I've lived among humans long enough, I understand their customs. I care about Aisha, and we are not playing by Xara's rulebook."

"Caring about her makes the mating sweeter, but she's still ours."

Liam dragged breath to the bottom of his lungs. When he blew it out, it was laced with smoke. Not only did he have to hash things out with his new mate, but his dragon needed a crash course in modernity.

"Not ours in the sense you believe her to be," he told the dragon. "This isn't Xara, nor is it the 1600s."

"I'm not going to like what you say next," the dragon warned. *"Think very carefully before you anger me."*

Liam pounded the steering wheel with a fist and pulled to the side of the dark, empty road. "The mating bite was your doing. A unilateral decision, I might add. Since you dove in with both wings and all your talons extended without discussing it with me, you may be stuck hearing something you don't like.

"My first priority is squaring things with Aisha. Once we get past the fallout from that, and perhaps a visit from her kinswoman, who will be furious, we may get to items like where the two of us will live."

"*Define 'may'.*" More smoke blasted from Liam's mouth.

"Aisha might be so put out at being deceived, she could tell me to get lost and never darken her door again."

"*She can't do that. She's ours.*"

"Aye, 'tis how you see it, but she is under no obligation to share your views." He thought back to what she'd said about the horses. "Her magic is bound up in her land and horses. I'm not sure exactly how it works, but she may not be able to leave—unless she can find a replacement to tend the power laced into the ranch."

"*But she won't have a choice. We're returning to Xara.*"

Liam didn't answer, but the hard truth was he was smitten. The mate bond cut both ways, and he'd do damn near anything to ensure Aisha's happiness.

Even if it meant he never saw Xara or any of his dragon kin again.

CHAPTER 9

The horses' restless ire blasted Aisha the second she turned her truck onto Colewright land. Victoria was there too, her magic burning even stronger than the horses' annoyance. For a moment, Aisha felt like a misbehaving teenager sneaking home after lying to her mom.

Except Charlotte never had this effect on her. Only Victoria could make her feel like a misbehaving fool.

She shook the uncomfortable, guilty feeling aside fast. If her grandmother was here in the flesh—and she'd bet her last saddle blanket she was—why the fuck hadn't she calmed the horses? That should get top billing.

Aisha had grown up hearing how the horses always

came first. Apparently, Victoria had decided the edict no longer applied to her.

She slowed the truck, toying with flipping a U and blasting out of the driveway. She'd never asked to be burdened with the Colewright legacy. Never signed on for being the Colewright witch glued to the land whether she wished it or not.

"I'm only as stuck as I want to be," she ground out.

The words were a revelation. Before tonight, the thought she might have options had never occurred to her. It made no sense. How could she live thirty plus years and not recognize she didn't have to do things just like every other Colewright witch who'd walked before?

She blinked as the world rearranged itself.

Victoria might poke holes in her newfound composure, but Aisha didn't think she'd be able to. She nosed the truck forward determined to get the worst of whatever faced her out of the way before Liam showed up.

Victoria wasn't his grandmother. She had no right censuring him, but that wouldn't stop her.

"She has no right condemning me, either." Aisha was still talking out loud. "Maybe when I was a kid, but I haven't been a kid for a long time."

The last few hundred yards of pot-holed driveway flashed beneath her tires. She'd barely pulled the truck to a stop and jumped down from the cab when Victoria stomped out of the kitchen door in the flesh, just as Aisha had suspected. No projections this time around. Her grandmother was probably too angry to sustain one.

"It's about fucking time," Victoria snarled. Before Aisha could reply that she didn't owe anyone any explanations—except maybe the horses who were whinnying up a storm—Victoria kept right on rolling.

"I told you to steer clear of that dragon shifter. I even paid Liam a visit. Did either of you listen to me? What happens next? Are you planning to leave the horses to fend for themselves? Do you have any idea what will happen to them if Colewright magic vanishes from this land?"

Aisha planted her hands on her hips and squared off in front of Victoria. "I suspect they'll end up 'normal' horses, not ones sensitive to magic. Besides, if you truly cared about them, you'd be in the barn, not out here treating me like a ten-year-old."

The whinnies escalated to squeals. The way the horses viewed things, she may have abandoned them, but she was home now, and they were flat out of patience. Aisha tossed her head. "You'll have to hang onto the rest of this lecture until I've calmed them down."

Mwrowwww! Hector raced from the shadows,

stopping a couple of inches in front of her, screeching and hissing.

"For Christ's sake, muffle whatever that creature is," she told Victoria before trotting into the barn.

The smells of horses and hay surrounded her as she shoved the sliding door aside and passed beneath the lintel into the barn. She grabbed carrots from the fridge and made the rounds of her babies, crooning to them, reaching into their minds and reassuring them she adored them. Her initial concern that Victoria would follow her inside didn't materialize. Perhaps her grandmother retained enough caring for the horses to understand they'd react badly to an argument unfolding right beneath their snouts.

Everyone bought her apologies but Butch. He was determined to hang onto his foul mood—even after taking three carrot bits from her.

Aisha couldn't spare any more time. Liam would be here soon, so she draped her usual magic around her charges and left the barn. Victoria stood where she'd left her. Hector was nowhere to be seen.

"Feel like a conversation between adults?" Aisha leveled her gaze at her grandmother.

"Not particularly." Victoria folded her arms beneath her breasts. "I specifically told you not to do something. You did it anyway."

"And you know this how?" Aisha took a step closer.

"Have you made it a habit to spy on me all these years?"

Victoria's nostrils flared. "You reek of sex."

"Maybe so, but you appear to be clear on who my partner was."

As always when she was cornered, Victoria switched tactics. "I care about you—"

Aisha rounded on her. "The hell you do. You care about tradition and Colewright witchery. I'm just the latest patsy in the string. Interesting that it's you here and not Mom. She was delighted when you faked your death and left. Not that she ever had much of a life, but those twenty years when it was just me and her were nice.

"Except for the cat. Take him with you. I do not need a resident mole."

"Hector isn't the point," Victoria shot back.

The distant rumble of a truck reached her. She straightened her shoulders. "Liam will be here soon. I—"

"Perfect. Gives me an opportunity to say what I need to once and be done with it."

Feeling bold, Aisha said, "What if I told you he was moving in here?"

Victoria's eyes narrowed to dangerous slits. "I'd forbid it. Only Colewright witches can live on these lands."

Aisha waved a dismissive hand. "Pfft. You made that up."

"I wouldn't be so sure of that. Why do you think you never knew your father?"

"Because you chased him away. As for whoever fathered Mom, hell you probably ate him as soon as he'd serviced you."

Anger streamed from Victoria, forming reddish ribbons around her tall, spare form. "Show some respect, young woman."

"Why?" Aisha tried to corral her fury, but it was a losing proposition. "Respect is a two-way street. If you flash your prickly side at Liam, I'll ask you to leave. I'm the Colewright witch in charge now. I'm the one with the link to the land."

Aisha couldn't believe she'd stood up to her grandmother. Thrown down the gauntlet. But she couldn't take the words back even if she wanted to, which she didn't. It was scary—and exhilarating—finally not to pick and choose what emerged from her mouth.

Liam's rattletrap truck rolled into view. He parked it next to hers and got out. With his superior magic, he must have sensed her grandmother. Good Victoria's presence hadn't chased him away.

Her respect for Liam expanded a notch. Not that she'd have expected him to back down from much, but knowing he'd be facing a pissed-off witch would give most anyone second thoughts.

He walked briskly to where she and Victoria stood facing each other. His coppery locks fell to his shoulders, and he wore the same denim she'd peeled off him a few hours before. With his broad-shouldered build and slim hips, he'd look good no matter what he chose.

He nodded briskly and wrapped an arm around her waist. "Top of the evening, ladies."

"Save your silver tongue," Victoria retorted. "Which part of 'stay away from my granddaughter' didn't sink in?"

He offered a disarming grin. "Guess her charms outplayed your prohibition."

Aisha caught wisps of a calming spell woven into his words. He was trying to defuse things, a path she'd trod many times with zero success.

"Someone cast the Heart's Desire spell tonight," Aisha told her grandmother, hoping to divert her from reading Liam the riot act.

"Aye, and not just any version," Liam chimed in. "'Twas the hardiest casting I've ever seen of that spell. The town green looked like the backroom in a bordello, with dozens of rutting couples."

Victoria narrowed her eyes farther. "Do you know

who was behind it? Summoning that casting at all is a violation of our covenant."

"Ha! You never gave up your seat on the sorcerer's council, did you?" Aisha stared at her grandmother.

"Why should I?" Victoria stared back. "Just because I left Stillwater was no reason to leave all my friends and associates behind." She shrugged. "Everyone magical knows I'm not dead."

"And everyone human wherever you're living now has no idea you're a witch," Aisha muttered.

"We don't know who was behind Heart's Desire." Liam circled the conversation back to Victoria's question.

"Don't you worry. I'll find out. Meanwhile"—she addressed her words to Liam—"my granddaughter is tied to this land. You're linked to Xara. You cannot take her away from these lands—or the horses."

"Why not?" Liam asked, curiosity underscoring his words.

"Because it will uproot her magic."

"You left," Aisha pointed out. A shaky, sinking feeling ran through her. Surely her grannie was blowing smoke, trying one more scare tactic to manipulate her.

Victoria nodded. "The land link passes from one witch to another, but only witches with Colewright blood qualify. I handed the baton to your mother. It freed me to leave. She gave it to you."

"When were you going to get around to telling me that little tidbit?" Aisha made a grab for her anger, but it bled out of her.

"That was Charlotte's job. I had no idea you didn't know." Victoria shook her head. "I'll be taking it up with her—soon."

Aisha sagged against Liam. She'd never heard this part of her family legacy. "But that's horrible," she ground out. "I'm a prisoner here."

"Not precisely. Once you produce a child, and she grows up, you'll be free to live whatever life you desire." Victoria looked from one to the other of them, seemingly satisfied her words had the desired effect. "I'm heading into town. I want to investigate that Heart's Desire mess before the energy fades, and I can't track who cast it."

Aisha started to offer up Arabia's name but decided against it. The longer Victoria was otherwise occupied, the better.

Light rose around her grandmother, and she shimmered into motes of brilliance before vanishing entirely.

Liam tightened his hold on Aisha. "I'm guessing you didn't know that wee bit about your magic."

Aisha shook her head, still reeling from the specter

of losing her magic if she walked away. "I don't get it," she muttered.

"Don't get what?" His voice was gentle.

"I leave to go into town. Tonight, I was gone for maybe six or seven hours. How the hell does the land know if I'm just leaving on an errand or moving elsewhere for good?"

Hector chose that moment to swoosh in from wherever he'd been hiding or hunting or whatever cats do in their spare time. Fangs bared, he launched himself at Liam, who let go of Aisha and caught him midair. The cat hissed, snarled, spit, and tried to swipe a paw with claws extended across Liam's hands.

Aisha made a grab for him, intent on making sure the cat didn't do any damage.

"Well, I'll be goddamned." Liam whistled long and low. "'Tis been many a long year since I've seen one such as him." He followed up with a string of Gaelic that froze Hector mid-swipe.

"Do you know what he is?" Aisha asked, feeling decidedly unsteady. The horses hadn't fussed one bit about the dragon shifter fifty yards from where they were bedded down, but Hector apparently viewed him as a threat.

"Och. Sure and 'tis a changeling." Liam angled his head, regarding Hector with interest.

"You have to say more than that."

"Changelings are faery children who were snared in spells when quite young. Sometimes faeries left their misbehaving spawn out on the Scottish moors to teach them respect. Other magic-wielders knew of the practice, and many would skulk on the moors at night waiting to snap up a faery child."

Aisha was fascinated. "But why? What did they use them for?"

"Various things. Apparently one of your witchy ancestors grabbed this one and imported him to the New World."

"I'm still not understanding why. From what I can see, Grannie uses Hector to spy on me, but surely she could accomplish the same thing with magic. Why imprison a harmless...?" She stopped talking at the grim expression on Liam's face.

"First off," he began and set the seemingly paralyzed not-a-cat on the ground, "faery spawn are far from harmless. They carry powerful magic. My guess is he's what locks you to these lands. I can't see any other rationale for having such a creature here."

Aisha sucked in a tense breath. It made sense. Her mother had hated the cat. Had she known what it was? "Is there some way to sever the enchantment?"

Liam nodded. "Aye, lass, that there is, and it would solve one problem."

Something about his tone flagged her attention.

"Does that mean there are others I don't know about?"

"'Tis exactly what it means. Can we go inside? Perhaps sit and have a wee dram of whiskey?"

"Um, sure." Trepidation dug sharp, icy claws into her spine as she led the way into the house.

Liam scooped up Hector before following her. "I'm not certain how long my immobilization spell will hold him. Do you have one of those animal crate things?"

"Yeah. Hang on." Aisha shut the door behind them and went to the laundry room, returning with a cat carrier.

Liam took it from her and set the comatose feline inside, latching the door.

"If his magic is powerful, how come he can't think himself free?" Aisha asked.

Instead of answering her, Liam glanced around her home. "Cozy. I like it." Walking to where liquor bottles lined a cabinet, he selected a bottle and poured whiskey into two glasses. "Come sit." He motioned to her, waiting until she settled onto one of two couches at right angles to one another.

Once she'd sat down, he sank onto the couch butting against hers so he faced her. "The changeling's magic is woven into the land. I suspect the system was set into place by one of your ancestors to ensure the witch du jour couldn't run off without paying the price of leaving her magic behind."

Aisha thought about it. "So, if my power is land-linked, and the changeling's is as well—"

"The land provides a conduit. If the changeling knows you're leaving, its task is to suck your power through that conduit." One corner of his chiseled mouth twisted downward. "Believe me, the changeling would be motivated. If it could lay hands on your power in addition to its own, it may well have enough to break free from the Colewright witches and be done with all of you."

"I can see where it would be a powerful incentive. I can't believe a faery would actually like spending its life as a cat. But what if one of us Colewrights snuck away? Once we were beyond the reach of these few acres, could the changeling's magic still grab ours? Beyond that, what would stop it from snapping up my magic anyway?"

"Honor is ingrained into their nature. As for your distance question, I don't know quite how that works," Liam replied. "What I am certain of, though, is that I possess sufficient magic to sever the creature's connection to these lands—and the Colewright witches." His direct gaze skittered away, and her stomach tightened. This must be the other thing. The one she didn't know about.

She drained half the whiskey in her tumbler, rewarded by it burning a hole in her throat as it slithered down. When she was through sputtering, she said, "Whatever this is, just tell me and have done with it."

He slugged back most of his whiskey, licking drops off his lips. Watching his tongue fascinated her. She remembered the wicked things it had done to her dark, private places, and the spot he'd bitten her shoulder tingled.

"Aye, lassie, 'tis the mate bond you're feeling." His brogue was thick as clotted cream.

"What mate bond?" Her voice was shriller than she would have liked.

"I'm a dragon shifter—"

She made a chopping motion. "I know that. What mate bond?"

"'Tis sorry I am we didn't have this conversation afore making love—"

"What conversation?" Her tone was decidedly shrill now. "You've told me less than nothing."

He held up both hands. "Let me get through this. I never will if you keep interrupting."

Aisha bit her tongue and spun one hand in a circle, urging him to get on with things. Maybe because Liam was distracted, Hector was waking up and yowling piteously. Now that she knew what he was, she felt sorry for him. No matter what came out of Liam's mouth in the next few minutes, she'd hold him to his promise to free Hector from bondage to the Colewright witches.

"You would have had a difficult time walking away from me once we made love," he began, "but my bondmate likes you." Liam swallowed, his throat working. "While we were consummating our lovemaking, he grabbed the point and bit you."

Aisha sent a pointed glance his way. "I don't understand what that means. I can go over there"—she pointed at a distant bookshelf—"and look it up, or you can tell me."

"It, uh, means you're my mate. And I'm yours," he hurried on. "Forever."

She fell back against the couch. "As in married with no possibility of divorce?"

He nodded. "You've put it in modern terms, but aye."

Fury boiled from her guts; she slammed a fist into the arm of the couch before bolting upright. Standing over him, she said. "Not just no. Hell no! I will not go from being a prisoner to this ranch to being imprisoned by some antiquated mate bond. I suppose that gives you the right to drag me back to Xara by my hair?"

Smoke billowed from Liam's mouth, followed by a gout of flame. She jumped back. Knowing what he was versus being confronted by direct evidence were two different animals entirely.

"Sorry." He stood too. "I'm sorry. It's my dragon. He's furious. His plan is for us to return to Xara, but for that you'd have to undergo a ritual transformation and become a dragon shifter."

"That's never, never going to happen. Tell your dragon to take a hike." She pressed her lips into a tight line. "Is there more, or have you told me everything?"

He nodded solemnly, steam still oozing from his mouth and nose. "A wee bit more. Ye're slated to love me forever. No other man will ever appeal to you." He held up a hand, probably at her horrified expression, and hurried to add. "The same is true for me. You're the only woman for me. Now and always. You can boot me out of here, tell me you never want to see me again, but that won't matter one whit."

He stopped long enough to take a breath. "The very last bit—"

"Awk. How could this possibly get any worse?" she demanded.

"Do you wish to hear or no?" At her tight nod, he went on. "I was banished from Xara for a hundred years. One of the requirements before I return is I must be mated, and—"

"Stop right there." She was so angry, her legs shook. "Everyone has deceived me. Grannie. Mom. You. Fuck!" Her skin crawled with revulsion and disgust at how everyone she'd ever cared about had used her.

"Is there aught I can do?" Pain laced through his words, but she didn't care. Let him hurt. He'd brought this on himself.

"Aye, laddie," she mocked him. "Free Hector, and then get the fuck out of here."

"As you wish." He bowed, a formal, old-fashioned gesture that spoke to how old he was.

The cat hissed and pawed at the cat carrier.

"Free him," Aisha screeched.

"Give me space to work."

She walked to the far side of the downstairs and watched while Liam wove gold and silver strands of power around the cat carrier before opening the door. Once he had Hector in his arms, he chanted in Gaelic so old she couldn't follow the incantation. The air around the cat took on an incandescent quality, and Hector's cat shape morphed into a cherubic faery with green and black wings and clouds of strawberry-colored hair.

The two-foot-tall creature threw its chubby arms around Liam's neck and kissed both his cheeks before flitting to the door and undoing the latch. Once it swung open, Hector—or whatever his name was—flew off into the budding dawn.

"What? No goodbye for me?" she taunted, feeling

bitchy and out of sorts.

A complex array of emotion played over Liam's gorgeous face. Resignation. Sorrow. Desire. "I'll be on my way, lass. As you requested. I am most humbly sorry, but I love you. I'll love you always. The mate bond doesn't lie. It picks our one true love."

"Yours, maybe," she muttered, feeling torn. Part of her wanted to run to him, throw herself into his arms, and never let go. Another part was horrified. To be driven by an amorphous dragon shifter mate bond that cut off the possibility of choice, of free will, was abhorrent.

As if to mock her, the bite on her shoulder burned like someone had poured liquid fire over the spot.

No, she corrected herself. *It's more like he branded me.*

To avoid dealing with any of it, she turned her back to Liam, listening as his heavy tread crossed to the door Hector had left open and continued on into her yard. It was only when she heard his truck engine turn over that she made her way to the door, shutting and locking it.

Hector was free. It meant she could leave, but desolation battered her. Hot, bitter tears underscored the sham her life had turned into, and she sank to the floor weeping and not understanding how everything had spun so far out of control.

CHAPTER 10

*L*iam did his damnedest to bury his feelings deep. Usually, it was easy for him to ignore his emotions, but not right now. Maybe if he'd eased into telling Aisha the truth, things would have gone better. Goddess's tits. Between her grandmother's offhanded disclosure and all the crap he'd tossed her way, no wonder she was devastated.

She had to be running way past the overload point.

He'd prodded and cajoled enough nervous clients up places that scared the stuffing out of them, and he knew better than to spew truth at folks who were already sucking fumes.

"Who am I kidding," he muttered. "She was already upset. If I'd pussyfooted around, titrated what I had to say, she'd have clawed my eyes out."

Despair scoured him, inscribing a path from his

belly outward. He didn't give a good goddamn about Xara. He wanted Aisha with a single-mindedness that shocked him. He'd never been one to go all mushy over a woman. It was why he'd put off finding a mate.

"This is your fault," he muttered, aiming the words at his bondmate.

A blast of steam filled the cab, fogging the windshield until Liam couldn't see out of it. He pulled off to the side of the road and opened a window.

"*I think not,*" the dragon countered. "*You picked her. You kissed her. You fondled her—*"

"Your point?" Liam broke in.

"*My point is I didn't bite her until you were about to claim her with your semen. That's part of the bond as well, or had you forgotten?*"

"She still could have walked away—absent your bite."

"*Not easily.*" The dragon paused for emphasis. "*If you're looking to blame someone, blame yourself. The question is, what are you going to do about it?*"

"Nothing. There's nothing I can do. You heard her. I disgust her. She ordered me out of her house. Her life. She—"

"*You bloody, fucking coward,*" the dragon snarled. "*I'm ashamed to be mated to you. We're dragons. Do you hear me? Dragons. We go after what we want. We don't slink away, defeated. If we go down, we go down bugling after we've fought as hard as we can."*

"I can't force her to love me," Liam protested.

"You don't have to. The mate bond has already done it for you."

A crafty note lined the dragon's message. Liam recognized it all too well. His dragon wouldn't stop badgering him until he'd done more than drive away from the Colewright ranch.

"Out with it."

"Out with what?" The dragon could have been the soul of innocence—if Liam didn't know his bondmate so well.

"An idea is percolating in that scaly head of yours. I'm not in the mood for guessing games."

His bondmate formed in his mind's eye, copper-green scales flashing as the dragon folded its wings across its back. *"Simple enough. The mate bond is in play, which links her to me as well. She's a horsewoman. She loves to ride. I say we take my form, fly back there, and offer to take her flying."*

"That's a horrible idea," Liam sputtered.

"Why? Give me one reason," the dragon persisted.

Liam winced. His bondmate was nothing if not stubborn. "It's daylight. Someone might see us."

"Not all the way out here. We're past human habitation. Haven't seen another car for at least a

league." The dragon paused for emphasis. *"What's your next excuse?"*

"It wasn't an excuse." Liam bristled. "Do you want someone to take photos of us and plaster them all over the Internet?"

"Certainly. Good lesson for those pesky humans. If they weren't such narrow-minded bastards—"

"Never mind," Liam broke in, knowing the dragon was about to start whining about how they never got to fly. "Bad question."

"If you don't like my idea, come up with your own. Driving back to our hoard and feeling sorry for yourself isn't an option. Neither is going climbing."

Those were exactly what Liam had been contemplating, but his bondmate was privy to all his thoughts. He shuffled through possibilities like a riverboat gambler who'd drawn a bad hand. The dragon remained silent. Maybe it knew there weren't many other choices.

He could drive back to the ranch, but he'd be lucky if Aisha would let him inside. He'd heard her twist the deadbolt lock once he started his truck. The biggest downside he saw with the dragon's plan was the horses might panic. Maybe. They'd probably never smelled a dragon, so it wouldn't be imprinted on their equine brains as something to fear or run from.

His chest felt hollow, empty. Would the unfulfilled

mate bond hound him forever? Surely, he wouldn't always feel this incomplete, like part of him was missing. He waited for a snarky comment from the dragon about how living with him would be a real pain in the arse, but the dragon, who was often into pithy lectures, didn't offer one.

Maybe showing up in his full dragon-esque glory was the right move. The way he was feeling, he couldn't sink much further. The worst thing that could happen would be someone might shoot at him, but his scales were impervious to bullets. He was past caring if his dual nature was outed. He could always leave town. Leave the country if need be. Go where no one knew him.

"You're stalling," the dragon observed.

He was. Liam slid the transmission back into gear and drove until he came to a side road full of potholes that looked as if no one had used it for years. He turned onto it and continued until the road petered out, maybe a couple of miles, and parked. Once out of the truck, he began removing his clothes, folding them neatly, and leaving them in the cab. He tucked the keys beneath a nearby pile of rocks.

Not that he was expecting anyone to bother the nondescript Chevy, but he was having second thoughts —third and fourth ones as well. What he was about to do was drastic. It would either work or blow up in his face. He gave the latter option maybe 70 percent, the former 30. If she cussed him out and chased him away a second time, he wouldn't return. Mate bond or no.

Standing in the chill air of early morning, bare feet solid on the rocky ground, he threw his magic wide open, inviting his dragon form. He'd picked a path, and by everything sacred, he'd follow it to its end. The dragon was right about it being very undragonlike to skulk away from Aisha. He craved her with a single-mindedness that meant as much to him as his hoard.

Probably more, if he were honest.

His bones cracked, lengthened, and shifted form; his skin changed to a scaly hide. His vision altered from human to dragon. Done procrastinating, he spread his wings and took to the skies. Damn but it felt good to be airborne. The familiar joy he garnered from his dragon form filled him.

Maybe this would work out. He loved his dragon so much, how could Aisha resist its primitive, arcane beauty? Dragons had been among the first creatures. They'd had all the worlds to themselves for millennia.

He gained height, scanning the land below. No humans. No ranches. The odd herd of cattle grazed, but they never even looked up, which boded well for the horses not going ape-shit nuts at his baked clay and rosemary smell. His human body oozed the same scent, but not nearly this strong.

He pumped his wings harder; smoke and fire belched from his mouth. The ranch came into view. Horses milled about the outdoor corral; Aisha was nowhere in sight. He scented the air, worried she might have given him the slip, used magic to whisk herself elsewhere, but she was inside.

A relieved breath rattled through him. Aisha was home, and the horses weren't bucking and squealing. It was the best he could hope for.

Should he bugle his presence?

Should he land?

What would maximize his chances of not angering her further?

He'd just opened his mouth to experiment with a short bugle when the front door flew open, and he felt like an idiot. She'd sensed him with her magic. Of course, she had.

Aisha shaded her eyes with a hand, staring skyward. An incredulous look twisted her face into an unreadable expression.

He started to ask her permission to land but thought better of it because he didn't want to offer her a chance to tell him to fuck off. Circling, he picked a spot close—but not too close—and folded his wings, furling them at the last minute to cushion his impact. Her scent reached him, the new-mown-hay smell delighting his senses.

Would she come to him? Or would they remain with fifty feet separating them until she resisted the mate bond's lure and shooed him away? He couldn't let that happen.

He bugled softly.

The horses trotted as close as they could get to the corral fence and whinnied a greeting. If Liam had been human, he would have laughed. At least the Colewright horses accepted him. Could he carve enough of a chink in their mistress's armor to allow the magnetism of the mate bond to grab her and draw her like a lodestone?

Right now, she was fighting it. If she gave in, she'd be lost—just like he was.

"*Aisha.*" He inclined his scaled head. Dragons bowed to no one, but he loved her.

"What are you doing back here?" she demanded.

"*I know you're angry—and you have every right to be—but would you like to go for a ride?*"

Her mouth gaped open. "On you?"

"*Who else?*"

He wove a subtle thread of magic into her mind. It was delicate enough, he hoped she wouldn't notice, but he had to know what she was thinking. Dragon possessiveness flowed, hot and compelling. It took all his self-control not to snatch her up and cradle her against his scaled chest.

If he did that, he'd never let her go.

"Bad idea," she said, tilting her chin at a defiant angle. "This mind-reading gig goes both ways."

"But you're so beautiful, and I want you so much." The words escaped before he could call them back.

Her stark expression softened, but not by much. "I understand why you came back, at least I think I do, but this will never work. Maybe there's some way out of your mate bond thing? You figured out how to free Hector. Surely, this isn't so very different."

If he read her tone correctly, she didn't sound hopeful he could break the enchantment so much as resigned she might be stuck with it. Her words broke his heart.

"I never wanted to hurt you."

"Yeah, Grannie would probably say the same thing. Good intentions don't go very far around here."

He walked closer and lowered himself onto his belly, so he was on a level with her. Steam billowed from his mouth, surrounding her. *"Why won't this work?"*

She ticked reasons off on her fingers. "One, I do not want to be a dragon shifter. Two, I have no intention of leaving Earth for Xara. Hell's bells, now that you broke the enchantment and I don't have to remain here, I have no idea what I want to do next."

"Would staying because you want to, not because

you have to make a difference?" He was genuinely curious.

Aisha nodded. "Of course. I do love my horses. They're innocent bystanders in this whole magical mess."

A chorus of whinnies rose from the corral as if they understood and agreed with her assessment of their virtue.

He blew out a gout of smoke, turning his head so he wouldn't choke her. *"The most important thing for me is being with you."* He picked his words carefully. *"And you being happy. If you never want to be a dragon shifter—or visit Xara—it's fine with me."*

Within him, his dragon shrieked imprecations. Liam scrambled upright just in time to divert the fire blasting from his mouth to a safe spot where it wouldn't burn any buildings.

"You're the one who sent me back here," Liam reminded his bondmate.

"Aye, to make sure she fills her role as our bondmate," the dragon shouted.

"All I hope is she'll give the mate bond a chance to weave its magic," Liam replied.

He focused his attention on Aisha, who'd no doubt heard the exchange. Before she could chase him and his overbearing bondmate away, he said, *"I meant that. Nothing would make me happier than for you to give us a chance. If I never return to Xara, I can live with that. My kinsmen are a bunch of sanctimonious prigs a lot of the time."*

He stopped talking long enough for more fire to blast skyward.

She smiled softly. "They can't be any worse than Grannie."

"Victoria is a piker by comparison. How about that ride?"

"Is it safe? Your dragon's pretty angry with me."

"Nay, 'tis me he's furious with for not acting like a sixteenth-century man and steamrolling over everything but my own needs."

"Do you want to return to Xara?" Her smile vanished, replaced by a serious expression.

"I thought I did, but that was before I mated with you."

She screwed her face into a frown. "Sounds like a politically correct reply if ever there was one."

"Maybe so, but in this particular case, I mean it with all my heart." He gathered his thoughts. *"When the council banished me, it was a relief. They have a lot of rules, many of which are holdovers from medieval times. At first, I missed being with other dragon shifters, but that faded."*

"When is the hundred years up?"

"Roughly ten years from now, and I admit I was

counting days and hours, ignoring the requirement I had to have a mate before I could return." He shrugged amid clanking scales. "'*Tis a strange thing to admit, but now that I have a mate, I'm not nearly as eager to go back to Xara.*"

The dragon thrashed from side to side within him. Clearly, this wasn't the outcome it envisioned, but at least it had stopped shoving fire out his gullet.

"*We can make our lives whatever both of us want, Aisha. Emphasis on both of us. If we can't agree, we'll keep talking until we do. For now, just being with you is everything I've ever wished for.*"

Longing streamed from her in bright waves. It gave him hope she'd give them a chance. Her face split into a shy smile. "I've always dreamed about flying, so I accept your offer."

"*All of it, or just the ride?*" He probably should have kept his mouth shut, but he needed to know.

"Let's begin with a ride." Her smile widened. "We can build on whatever happens from there."

It was good enough for him. His heart cracked wide open and overflowed with tenderness. Bending, he scooped her up with his forearms and hugged her before turning to deposit her on his broad back.

"*Grab hold of the two horns at the base of my neck,*" he instructed.

She laughed, and it made his soul light up with

love. "I've broken lots of broncs," she said. "I'm sure I can manage this."

She was still laughing when he spread his wings, pumping hard until they were airborne. He dipped and banked, letting her get a feel for how to shift her weight to remain astride. Once he felt certain of her skill, he grew bold, climbing steeply, and then plummeting, only to pull out of the dive at the last minute.

"I love that," she yelled into the slipstream. "Do it again."

Liam snorted steam. There were a whole lot of activities where he wanted her to utter those three words. Joy swelled within him. She was giving them an opportunity for the seeds of love to grow and flourish.

"Thank you."

"For what?" She wound her arms as far around his thick neck as she could reach, breasts pressing into his spine.

"Being you. Ready to land, lass?"

"Maybe." She drew out the word. "Do you have something in mind that requires landing?"

"Indeed, I do. I want to take you to bed and not get up until both of us are good and ready."

"We may never leave my bedroom."

"Och, 'tis a fate worse than death, but you've twisted my arm."

"I love it that you have a sense of humor."

"And I love you."

He circled, intent on landing. Anticipation of loving her thrummed through every cell. He glided to a stop in front of the ranch house and helped Aisha to the ground before calling shift magic. Once he'd shimmered back into his human form, he was a little embarrassed to see his cock jutting from his body.

Being ready was one thing, but at least if he'd had clothing on, it would have hidden some of the damning evidence of how hot she made him.

She threw her arms around his neck, and he hugged her tight. "Come on." She disentangled herself and led the way inside, shucking clothing as soon as she got the door shut. "You're ahead," she said, sounding breathless. "You started out naked."

"Nay, lassie, we're both ahead because we have each other." Lifting her half-dressed body into his arms, he carried her up the ladder. This would be their first coupling as a mated pair, and he couldn't wait.

She wriggled out of his arms and sat cross-legged on the bed, her eyes liquid with desire. "You're thinking. I feel the wheels turning."

"About you, sweetheart. Together, we're invincible. Dragons. Grandmothers. Demanding horses. We'll tackle them as they happen." He launched himself at her, tumbling her onto her back. Just before he kissed her, he added, "The only thing I want to tackle right now, though, is you."

"I like a man with strong priorities, particularly when one of them is me."

It was a good time to stop talking, so he crushed his mouth over hers.

EPILOGUE

Three Months Later

Aisha ran her hands down her hips, smoothing the ivory silk one more time. She was afraid to sit in case her dress wrinkled. Today had dawned bright, clear, and cold. According to her tarot spreads, it was the most auspicious day for her wedding to Liam. Anticipation made her heart beat faster. The mate bond was one thing, but she'd always dreamed of being married. Never mind it was a silly human custom.

She longed for Liam's presence, but he was nowhere to be seen. Victoria and Charlotte had chased him away the previous night with firm instructions he couldn't return until right before the ceremony. Dragon possessiveness had shaded his green eyes to a smoldering amber she recognized from their lovemaking, but he'd nodded pleasantly and driven away.

Probably back to the miner's cabin—and his hoard. When he'd shown it to her, she'd been fascinated by the piles of gold, antique silver, and gemstones tucked deep in an old mineshaft. They were keeping both her ranch and his cabin—at least for now. Someday, they might move away from Stillwater, but not anytime soon.

She had her horses. He had his guide business. But most importantly, they had each other.

The ranch house was decked out with candles. Flowers were too hard to come by this time of year, so she'd substituted fragrant herbs, pine boughs, and holly berries. Making peace with Victoria had taken weeks. If her grannie hadn't been immersed in dealing with the Heart's Desire spell fallout, it might have taken far longer.

Hector's freedom had diverted her too. While Charlotte had whooped, cheered, and muttered, "Good riddance," at hearing Hector was free, Victoria was horrified.

It had taken both her and Liam to convince Victoria you couldn't hold someone against their will with magic, unless you wanted them to resent you forever. Victoria's only argument had been they'd always done it this way, but even she understood history wasn't sufficient reason to maintain a practice that had lost its effectiveness.

Spreading her arms, Aisha spun in a circle, inhaling the rich scents of pine, sage, and rosemary. She'd sent the other Colewrights to town ostensibly for last minute items, but more to get away from her mother's and grannie's constant bitching and bickering. One of the sideline consequences of the Heart's Desire spell was it blew the lid off the secrecy shrouding magic from humans—and magic wielders from one another.

She chuckled. Witches, shifters, mages, Fae, and everyone else with magic had finally crawled out from under their "don't ask, don't tell" policy. Because humans knew about magic, both her mother and grandmother had been able to pop back up.

No one said much of anything about them being dead. As might be expected, some humans fared better knowing about the supernatural world than others. A few remained in deep denial, but no one challenged them. It was a big revelation to wrap your mind around.

Change would take time. Maybe as much as a generation but kicking the closet door open was a critical step. All the skeletons had fallen out. It wasn't surprising some were still rattling louder than others.

Whinnies blasted her from the barn. The horses

knew today was special, and they wanted to share her joy. Aisha glanced at her pristine gown. It wouldn't look nearly as lovely covered in horse slobber, so she grabbed a full-length cloak from the hall tree and draped it around her shoulders, fastening it down the front. She traded her shoes for boots.

Strands of hair tickled her face, and she tucked them behind her ears, careful not to disturb the elaborate braids her mother had worked on for over an hour earlier in the day. After a final inspection to reassure herself everything was perfect, and her work was done, she walked out into the yard. All the puddles had a thin sheet of ice over them. The temperature hadn't cracked freezing for weeks.

Her herd sensed she was moving toward them; the horsey sounds escalated. Aisha let herself into the barn and grabbed the treat bag from the ancient refrigerator. She chatted with her charges as she handed out apples and pears. Butch head butted her, and she scratched between his ears. He leaned into her touch.

Liam had taken to riding the stallion, and Butch adored him. "That's what you needed." Aisha kept on scratching. "A man to bond with."

The horse snorted his agreement and filched another chunk of pear with his squared-off teeth.

"How about it?" She tossed the question out to everybody. "Want to go outside?"

Excited neighs almost deafened her. The horses all had their winter coats and were thick and shaggy. They loved rolling in snow almost as much as dogs did. She slid the barn's back door open, allowing access to a large corral. The horses charged through, milling around the yard. She broke open a hay bale and scattered it in the feed tough. Their drinking tub had a small heating element to keep the water from freezing, and she checked to make certain it was working.

Satisfied she'd done all she could for her charges, she backtracked. Before she made it to the house, a blast of familiar magic closed from above her. Aisha stared, certain she'd been mistaken, but the strawberry-haired changeling flew toward her, wings beating so fast they were a blur.

"Hector?" The name stuck in her craw, and she cleared her throat.

The sprite pushed hair away from its face with both chubby hands. "That's who I was," it announced, "but my real name is Mariana."

"You're female?"

"State the obvious, why don't you?" The changeling was only a few feet away.

"Sorry. It was a stupid comment, but you surprised me. I didn't expect I'd ever see you again."

The changeling landed on her shoulder. "What's broken can't be put back together. I'm safe enough."

"Well, um, it's nice to see you." Aisha tried for polite. Today was her wedding day, and she refused to hold grudges or wish anyone ill. After all, none of Mariana's imprisonment had been her fault.

"Ha! Now there's a prime piece of bullshit. No love lost between the two of us, missy, but I always liked you."

"Good to know." Aisha ducked into the house after a particularly vicious blast of wind rustled through the tight weave of her cloak.

Mariana jumped down, softening her landing with extended wings, and turned in a circle, inspecting the ranch house. "Didn't change much, I see. Where is that wonderful man?" Her voice took on reverential tones.

"He'll arrive soon. We're getting married."

Mariana clasped her hands together. "I know. It's why I'm here. I heard about it in town. You know," she hurried on, "that love spell that went tits up was such a blessing. Not that people don't look twice at me, but some of them chalk me off as someone who didn't grow quite right. Others, they kind of look the other way, but I'm free.

"Free to do what I want. Free of you Colewrights. I—"

Aisha started to laugh as she divested herself of her cloak and hung it back on its hook. "I liked you better as a cat. You weren't nearly as chatty." She levered off her outdoor boots.

The changeling bristled, drawing herself up to her full two-foot height. "Never say that." She stamped her foot. "Never. You have no idea how I suffered. I hated being a cat. Hated it. And it went on forever." Pain and desolation laced through her words.

Aisha crouched low and opened her arms. Mariana barreled into them, and Aisha held her close, no longer worried about her dress in the face of the changeling's palpable anguish. "I'm sorry," she murmured. "I had no idea. If I'd known, I'd have searched for a spell to free you myself."

"Wouldn't have worked," Mariana snuffled. "Your magic was bound up with mine. It would have hurt you to free me."

The door swung open, and Liam strode through, pushing it shut behind him. Resplendent in pure-white hunting leathers blazoned with runes symbolic of his dragon shifter power, he was stunning. Knee-high buff-colored boots laced up his calves.

Mariana let go of Aisha and raced to him, winding her arms around his legs. "I wondered if we'd see you again," he said as he lifted her until she rode on his shoulders.

"You freed me." The same reverence and wonder

she'd displayed earlier wove through her words. "How could I not offer wedding blessings?"

"Thank you, little one." Liam's tone was serious.

She bobbed her head. "Welcome. I don't miss being a cat, but I miss living here. It was cozy."

"You can visit anytime you want," Aisha told her. "And if you wanted to move back in, we'd find a spot for you."

"Really?" The changeling brightened.

"Truly," Liam reassured her and strode to Aisha's side. "How's my bride?"

She let her gaze rove over him, drinking him in. His tawny hair had been drawn into a queue that rode low on the base of his neck, and his green eyes sparkled with merriment. With his hair drawn back from his face, the clean, spare lines of forehead, cheeks, and chin made him Greek-god gorgeous.

"I'm fine," she informed him. "And about this close"—she held her thumb and index finger about an inch apart—"to dragging you upstairs and making our guests wait."

"A woman after my own heart." He wrapped his arms around her. Mariana bent forward, hugging her too, and Aisha remembered the cat's decidedly voyeuristic side.

"My grandmother will be back soon—" Aisha

began about the time the door Liam had just shut flew open.

Mariana skinned her lips back from her teeth and hissed.

"None of that." Aisha leveled her gaze at the changeling. "Not on my wedding day."

Charlotte dragged several bags inside. "Everything under control, dear?" she inquired brightly, but her smile slid into a frown when she saw Liam. "What are you doing here? It's bad luck to see your bride before the ceremony."

"I just got here." Soothing magic underscored Liam's words. "I thought Aisha might need some help. Besides, everyone will begin arriving soon, and they're my guests too."

Seemingly mollified, her mother began unpacking bags and setting food items out on serving plates.

Victoria trudged inside, similarly burdened, and kicked the door shut. A good thing since the temperature inside was dropping fast. She dropped the bags and straightened, staring right at Mariana. "You have a lot of nerve." She shook a finger at the sprite.

"Ha. Pot. Kettle," Mariana shot back. "Who imprisoned whom, huh? Witch."

"Now, look here. Both of you." Aisha stepped between them. "This is my wedding day. I will not have any heated words beneath my roof. Got it?"

"She started it," Mariana said sullenly.

"I don't care who started it. Any animosity ends now." Aisha dropped a hand on Victoria's shoulder.

The older woman shrugged her hand off and bent to the sacks she'd dragged inside, removing items and arranging them in logical order on the laden tables lining the room. It was as close to acquiescence as Aisha was likely to get, but at least Victoria wasn't baiting the changeling anymore.

Liam set Mariana down. "What can I do?" he asked.

"Nothing," Aisha told him. "Wait for our guests. And the local preacher who was skittish as a colt when he agreed to marry us."

Liam shrugged. "To him, I suppose we're still manifestations of evil."

"What do we do if he doesn't show up?" Worry beat a path through her. If she was going to spin a coercion spell, she should have had it in place long before now. Those types of enchantments needed time to simmer.

"I'll marry you," Victoria said.

Aisha waited for her grandmother to add it was against her better judgement, that Aisha shouldn't be marrying at all, but if she had to tread that path, it should be handfasting with another witch. But Victoria didn't launch into the litany she'd delivered so many times, Aisha knew it by heart.

Liam's head snapped up. "Son of a bitch."

"What?" Aisha, her mother, and grandmother all asked in unison.

"Dragon shifters are on their way, lots of them if the feel of their magic is any indication." He broke into a broad smile. "I invited my kinsmen, never dreaming any of them would leave Xara."

Aisha wove an arm around his waist. "I'm happy for you."

"Be happy for us. They'll bless our mating bond—and our union." He took a measured breath. "I can't recall when any of my kin left Xara, willingly, that is."

Aisha sent magic spiraling outward. Now that she knew what to look for, the faint thrum of power she associated with Liam pricked her. She also heard the distant roar of automobiles.

Everyone would be here soon.

Her mother folded the paper grocery bags, stashed them under the sink, and shrugged out of her coat. Victoria removed hers too.

Aisha moved to where her kinswomen stood and wrapped her arms around them both. "I do love you. You've always wanted the best for me, and I appreciate everything you've done, even if I didn't agree at the time."

"Really?" Charlotte's hazel eyes developed a suspicious sheen. "Even though I never told you about Hector and the land-spell?"

"Really," Aisha reassured her. "If you'd been able to find a way, you'd have told me."

"Pfft." Victoria waved a dismissive hand but stopped before her other lecture about their strain weakening emerged.

Liam trotted to the door and pulled it open. Buck-naked men and women strode inside, chattering excitedly in Gaelic. They hugged Liam, kissing both his cheeks. He beckoned to her, and Aisha hurried to his side, greeting his kin. Mariana fluttered from one dragon shifter to the next. All of them embraced her and made much of her, clearly delighted by her faery presence.

"I love it that you're here for Liam," she told the dragons. "Our other guests will be here very soon. Is there, um, any way you might cast a glamor, and uh...?"

"Och, aye," a tall, silver-haired dragon shifter said. "Humans will be here, and you want us clothed." He snapped two fingers, and magnificent garb from straight out of the eighteenth century materialized, draping him in velvet and brocade.

Aisha guessed that was when he'd left Earth for Xara.

The other dragon shifters picked up on his cue,

amid the rustle of fabric, about the time a staunch knock battered the door.

Victoria crossed the room, opening it to a stream of guests who just kept on coming until the ranch house was packed with humans and every shade of magic-wielder imaginable. Liquor flowed as people offered toasts.

The only one missing was the preacher.

Victoria sidled close. "Want me to take over?" she asked.

"Maybe so," Aisha replied. "Hang on. Let me talk with Liam and see what he wants to do."

He was in the center of a circle of dragon shifters, obviously catching up on the last ninety years. "Aye, love?" He drew her into an embrace.

"Preacher got cold feet," she told him. "Are you good with Grannie marrying us? It will be a witch ceremony."

"I have an idea"—the silver-haired dragon shifter smiled—"if you approve, of course. In our society, the mate bond is sufficient, but we have not forgotten human customs. Since you're a witch, and your intended is one of us, I would join with your grandmother in performing the ceremony. It will be the beginnings of good will between our people."

Aisha swallowed hard. Would Victoria go along

with what was a very reasonable suggestion? "I'll ask her."

"No need." Victoria's contralto rang from behind her. "Give the dragon shifter and me a few minutes, and we'll be ready to begin." She crooked a long-nailed index finger, and the dragon followed her to a corner of the room where they stood, heads bent together.

Aisha took Liam's hand. "Let's stand over by the altar, so we'll be ready when they are." They threaded their way through the overcrowded room amid toasts and wishes for a long and happy life together. She stopped in front of the spot where she'd cast her spells.

"This is where it all began," she murmured to Liam.

"What do you mean?" he asked.

"Silly." She leaned into him. "It's where I ginned up the love charm that started everything."

He kissed her forehead. "We need to turn it into a shrine, sweetheart. You've made me the happiest man alive."

Before she could reply, Victoria and the dragon shifter walked toward them, wine goblets in hand. The next few minutes passed in a blur as Aisha listened to her grandmother call to the four seasons and four directions while she walked them through a traditional handfasting ceremony.

While their hands were still bound with red rope, the dragon shifter picked up a small knife from a table behind him. "Hold out your hands," he instructed and made a small, deep incision in both their thumbs. Once their blood flowed together, he barked a word in Gaelic, and the wounds closed as if they'd never been there.

"We pronounce you husband and wife," Victoria raised her voice to be heard throughout the room.

"Aye," the dragon shifter chimed in, "through this life and all others to come." He nudged Liam. "What are you waiting for, mate? Kiss your bride."

Liam laughed and swept her into a hug, slashing his mouth atop hers.

Aisha clung to him, kissing him back. Happiness boiled through her, so sharp and fierce, she'd have taken on the world if it had the temerity to step between her and her mate.

And now her husband too.

Music began to play. People must have brought instruments. Aisha could have kissed Liam forever, but for now she let go and turned to face the crowd. Together, they greeted their guests.

When the reception line finally thinned, Liam bent toward her. "I have good news. My kinsmen have decided to end their self-imposed separation."

"They're leaving Xara?" Aisha asked, incredulous.

"Not exactly, but they'll come and go from now on."

"What changed their minds?" she asked.

He shrugged. "I guess it was me. They expected me to fail miserably living among humans. When I didn't show up begging them to take me back, it proved one of us could survive in a human world."

"And if one of you could do it…" she began.

"Exactly, my brilliant witch. How soon do you think we could get out of here? I booked us the honeymoon suite in town."

"Aw, sweetie, you didn't."

"'Fraid I did. Can your mom or grannie look out for the horses for a couple of days?"

"We can, and we will." Charlotte closed from one side and made shooing motions. "Get moving. Victoria and I will take care of everything here." She hugged Aisha, and Aisha returned her embrace.

"I love you, Mom."

"I know you do, honey. Love you back, just as much." She melted into the crowd.

"How do you want to do this?" Liam asked.

"What do you mean? We'll get the truck keys and drive into town. After I've packed a few things."

"We could teleport? It's faster. Cleaner. From here right into our room." He smiled engagingly. "You might already have a few things there. I got busy after your mother and grannie chased me out of here yesterday."

She linked an arm through his. "Perfect. Let's do it. Do you need to say goodbyes, first?"

"Eh, if I do that, we'll be here all night. Dragon shifters are a bunch of raconteurs at heart."

Aisha tightened her grip on him, feeling his magic boil around them. The walls of her home fell away, replaced by the antique furnishings of Empire House, the oldest, fanciest hotel in town.

"Wow. You weren't kidding about the honeymoon suite." She twirled in place taking in a bed with an intricately carved headboard that rose six feet in the air.

"Nothing but the best for you, sweetheart. Now and always." Love spilled from him, surrounding them both.

Her throat thickened. "I love you."

"I know, but I never get tired of hearing it." He placed his hands on her shoulders. "Can I start on all those hundreds of little buttons holding this dress in place?"

She giggled. "Not hundreds, but there are plenty of them. It's a time-honored tradition to keep the groom's lust at bay."

"What about the bride's?" he teased.

"Oh, we're not that way at all," she teased back.

A playful gleam illuminated his eyes, giving them a mossy sheen. "Oh, really? We'll see about that." Taking a few steps back, he unlaced his leather shirt, tugging it over his head. The low light of the room danced over the planes of his body, illuminating it until he became so profanely beautiful she couldn't look away.

When he started on the laces of his trousers, she made a dive for him and toppled them across the bed, intent on finishing undoing his pants.

"You'll muss your dress," he told her.

She hiked up the skirts. "I don't care. Make love with me. We'll figure out the dress later."

"Whatever milady desires." His rich laughter inflamed her as he bent to do her bidding.

You've reached the end of *Branded*, one of the books in That Old Black Magic series. Be sure to check out all the others.

Please, please leave a review for *Branded*. Do it now, while it's fresh in your mind. Doesn't have to be fancy.

A sentence or two works fine.

If you enjoyed *Branded*, you may like some of my other supernatural novellas. Samples from *Shadows in Time* and *Heart's Flame* follow, so just keep right on reading!

ABOUT THE AUTHOR

Ann Gimpel is a USA Today bestselling author. A lifelong aficionado of the unusual, she began writing speculative fiction a few years ago. Since then her short fiction has appeared in a number of webzines, magazines, and anthologies. Her longer books run the gamut from urban fantasy to paranormal romance to science fiction. Once upon a time, she nurtured clients. Now she nurtures dark, gritty fantasy stories that push hard against reality. When she's not writing, she's in the backcountry getting down and dirty with her camera. She's published over 65 books to date, with several more planned for 2018 and beyond. A husband, grown children, grandchildren and wolf hybrids round out her family.

Keep up with her at www.anngimpel.com or http://anngimpel.blogspot.com

If you enjoyed what you read, get in line for special offers and pre-release special reads. Newsletter Signup!

A disgruntled heiress and a sexy Scottish laird are drawn together by a determined ghost whose love—and magic—reach beyond the grave.

Siobhan Macquire looked for the right man all her life —someone who'd love her, not her money. Heiress to a whiskey fortune, she attracted a string of men out to drain her for everything they could get. Her last boyfriend was no exception. Despondent about being used—again—she goes for a walk in the Highlands to think things through, determined to alter her pick-a-loser pattern.

She wanders alone for hours with the weather steadily growing worse—except there don't seem to be any nearby villages anymore. Soaking wet and scared, she's relieved when someone calls out to her, and a stunning man emerges from the mist. Except when she looks closer, there's a whole lot wrong. His kilt is way too long, and he talks with an archaic accent.

Is it possible she's not only lost in the countryside, but also in time?

Scottish Highlands, 1790

Aidan MacTavish slogged over boggy ground, making his way into the hills behind his castle. Power cloaked him, glowing blue-white against the storm-dark day, but he didn't bother to hide himself. He might frighten the odd villager, but chances of meeting anyone on his lands were thin, and his own servants and cottagers were used to his magical ability. All the folk on his lands were free to leave any time. Though some owed him service, he never balked at turning them loose if his magic frightened them.

Rain pelted from the skies, and he wrapped a thick, woolen plaid closer about his torso from habit. The cold and rain didn't bother him. In truth, he needed respite from the fire urging him from within. The land steepened beneath his boots, and he made his way around rocks onto a precipitous track leading to a shrine hidden high up the mountainside.

He knew when he married Moira it wasn't wise. Fae blood—the blood of the Sidhe—ran strong in her veins, and she struggled to keep one foot in the land of the living. Her people never approved of her marrying a mortal, so they did their damnedest to lure her from his side. He'd found her often enough, trapped in a vision or a dream, and it took cunningly woven magic to draw her back.

The pain in her silver eyes haunted him, and he supposed it always would. Despite knowing children with a mortal might be her undoing, she'd insisted they try—to keep the MacTavish line alive. Aidan was the last of three brothers, so he hadn't taken a firm enough stand.

After multiple miscarriages and a stillbirth, his misgivings shifted to alarm. When he refused her body, she used magic to beguile him, certain the next pregnancy would take. He never could bring himself to erect warding against her charms, something he'd blamed himself for over and over.

She finally slipped beyond where even he could call her back.

Though she'd carried a child long enough for it to live outside her body, childbirth was her undoing. She lost so much blood, she'd faded into the *Dreaming*—

world of the Fae—never to return. At least not in the flesh.

God knew she haunted his dreams often enough.

Their son only lived a matter of hours. Too much Fae, not enough human, to survive in either world. Moira realized the wee bairn had no chance, and she'd whispered how sorry she was over and over in her archaic form of Gaelic before she was no more. Gone in a burst of iridescent light that scarred his corneas with her passing. Lost in grief, he'd barely given a passing thought to his sight when it returned.

Aidan shook water out of his eyes—and himself out of the past—and kept climbing. Half an hour more and he'd be where he could raise Moira, ask what she wanted, why she wouldn't leave him to grieve and move beyond the pain of not having her by his side.

The villagers had been spooked by her disappearance. At least his son resided in a tiny coffin tucked away in the family graveyard, but the absence of Moira's body sent many of his cottagers into a frenzy of signs against evil and muttered imprecations. Enough had left that this past planting season required magic in lieu of braw strength.

At least there'd be enough food to nourish everyone through the winter. For a while, he hadn't been certain, but the crops in the fields looked robust. It had taken still more magic, but enough cut peat blocks to warm the huts were stacked in several outbuildings.

He rounded a final rocky outcropping and slipped into the cave he used for rituals. The scents of burned heather and expended magic—replete with the tang of the sea—filled his nostrils and brought him a measure of peace. Calling a mage light, he tossed crumbled peat into the central fire pit. Fire blazed to his summons and steam rose from his soaked plaid.

Aidan took a moment to center himself, balanced his earth-based Druid power, and cast his gaze about the familiar space. A dozen paces round, it was the entryway to a tunnel system leading deep into the mountain. Rocks studded the dirt walls, and he'd constructed a fire pit in the precise center to concentrate his ability. Runic markings to strengthen his arcane skills even further were scattered strategically.

The cave suited his special brand of power and enhanced his magic in the best possible way. He'd avoided it since Moira's death, afraid he'd batter himself senseless trying to get into the *Dreaming*—a land barred to humans.

Aidan clasped his hands behind his back and began the incantation to summon his dead wife back from the other side. He couldn't go the remainder of his life with her visiting his dreams, exhorting him in

Gaelic to do something he couldn't decipher, not because he didn't speak the language, but because her words made no sense.

Nay. He needed peace.

More important, so did she. Was she captive in the veil between the worlds? If that was the problem, it couldn't be comfortable for her. Her kinfolk should've come to her aid, but mayhap they were still angry with her for leaving the fold.

He poured power into his working until the air around him crackled with sparks and took on a burnt smell, different from his fire.

"Moira," he called. "Moira, love. Come to me. Talk with me."

Nothing.

Aidan pulled more magic, digging deep into the earth that mothered his gift. He filled himself until every mote of his being was ablaze with light, until if he took on any more power, he'd burst into a million particles of light, and called again.

The air on the far side of his smoldering peat fire developed an incandescent quality.

"Aye, lass," he urged. "That's the way of it. Come through. I'll see you back safe."

"I know ye will, love." Moira took shape, red hair falling to her knees and silver eyes glowing in the fire's reflection. She held out spectral arms, and Aidan's heart stuttered in his chest.

He wanted to go to her, crush her against him, but that wouldn't help either of them. "Tell me what ye need, Moira. I see you in my dreams. Hell, I see you if I so much as shutter my eyes for the barest moment."

She nodded, making her hair flutter about her. "Och aye, mo croi, 'tis sorry I am."

"Are ye trapped? Can I sing you through to the *Dreaming*?" He sought a balance point, where he could hold his spell and maintain enough sentience to talk. It wasn't easy with the amount of magic pouring through him.

"Nay, love, but 'tis kind of you to ask. 'Tis why I fell in love with you, Aidan. Ye were the kindest, most compassionate man I'd ever known." Sorrow spilled from her in silver waves, almost the same shade as her eyes.

"I love you too, lass. Likely I always will, but ye canna live in the world of men, and I canna bide in the *Dreaming*. What would ye have me do?"

"Ye'll meet a lass. Ye must take her to wife. 'Tis what I've been trying to tell you, yet ye rarely leave your lands. Ye must rejoin the world, or what I've seen willna come to pass."

Shock battered him, and his spell faltered. He

gathered it before it vanished entirely and Moira along with it. "How is it ye see into the world of men?"

She shrugged. "How can any of us do what we do with our power?"

"Can ye pierce the veil into the *Dreaming*?" he asked again, still worried she might be stuck between the worlds.

"Aye, love. It costs me dear, though, each time I return to infuse sense into that thick noggin of yours."

Aidan inhaled raggedly. The power sluicing through him turned him into a vortex, only partly human, mostly spirit. "I promise I'll keep my eyes open for this lass ye mentioned."

"I canna ask for more. Let me go, Aidan. When I come on my own, 'tisn't near as draining."

He gradually loosed his spell—needing some power to remain upright—and Moira faded, along with her familiar, loving energy that had nurtured him so long. He'd met her when he wasn't much more than half-grown. Like all Fae, she was ageless, and she'd teased him that she had to wait for him to grow up before she threw herself into his arms.

"Enough!" he thundered to the air alight with energy.

The spoken word took him by surprise. Damn it, anyway! He hadn't asked her to leave him be, so both of them could get beyond her death. How could he have forgotten something so basic?

Truth slapped him. Her magic trumped his by a hundredfold, a thousand, and she hadn't wanted him to say it. A crooked smile formed, and he commanded his fire to extinguish itself.

A lass, eh? He didn't totally believe Moira's prediction, but if it turned out to be true, hopefully she'd be warm, kind, compassionate. Good she'd have Moira's blessings. Aidan hated to even consider what hell any woman he sparked an interest in might go through—if Moira disapproved of her.

He walked outside into rain even worse than when he'd arrived at the sacred cave. At least his plaid was drier, but it wouldn't be for long. The bleakness surrounding him since Moira and their son's deaths cracked. Hope leached into his heart as he made his way back along the dicey trail, slipping and sliding on stones dislodged by water.

A glance at the cloud-filled sky reassured him it was still afternoon. He'd go for a ride on the moors, into the heart of the power that fueled his Druid magic. Once there, he'd send the horse home. A walk into Inverness would do him good, followed by a meal at one of the common houses. He could summon transport come morning to make his way back to his holdings.

A jaunty tune bubbled past his lips. Moira was right about one thing. He'd stayed far too close to home since her death. The specter of going out for a bit invigorated him, made him remember what it felt like to be a man. He quickened his pace for home. After a time, its turrets and towers came into view.

"Ye've returned then, Laird." His stableman's voice broke into Aidan's reverie, and the tall, spare man loped out of the mist. "Ye're soaked. I'll instruct the housekeeper to draw you a hot bath."

"Aye, I have indeed returned, and in more ways than one. I'll not be wanting that bath, though. Saddle Soulna for me."

"Ye needna see to the cottagers. I sent my lad not one day since." Robert MacConough sounded solicitous, and it smote Aidan that his people felt the need to coddle him.

Aidan clapped him on the back. "'Tis grateful I am for all ye've done, but I've mourned long enough. Time for me to take care of things again."

"Truly, Laird?" Robert's weather-beaten face broke into a broad grin.

"Truly. Doona stand there gawking. My horse."

"Of course, Laird. Right away." Robert turned toward the stables then took off at a brisk trot.

"Doona be surprised if he returns without me," Aidan called after him. "I'll ride into the moorlands, then be sending him along. And I'll be spending the evening in Inverness."

"As my laird wishes," drifted to him in the soggy air.

Aidan breathed deep. Scotland. No place like it. He'd lived half a life this past year. Not much he could do about those lost months, but he'd be damned if he'd retreat to the shadows again. They'd dogged his heels for far too long. He'd always love Moira, but it was past time to move forward.

Scottish Highlands, Modern Time

Sam pulled the draw cords of her hood tighter, squinting against driving rain. She shivered and willed her legs to move faster. Even in the northern latitudes, it got dark eventually during what passed for summer, and the light was definitely fading. She stumbled, and one foot sloughed into a hole. Cursing roundly, she yanked it out, pissed that the mud added what felt like ten pounds to her tired leg. Going on a ramble—as the locals called it—by herself seemed like a good idea earlier in the afternoon. Now she wasn't so sure. Hours had passed since she'd seen another soul.

The air felt heavy—and threatening, somehow.

"Don't be ridiculous," she scolded herself. "My imagination's off the clock, working overtime."

A flash toward the river was followed almost immediately by a rumbling crash. The sky lit again, casting the wet greenery and surrounding mountains in a macabre glow. Thunder exploded, so loud it made her ears ring. The next lightning flare sparked off a rock not twenty feet away. Unrelenting rain pelted her.

Sam's heart sped up. She stared at the mountains ringed about her. Why wasn't the storm up there? Lightning was supposed to be drawn to high points, not meadows saturated with water.

As if determined to prove her wrong, another flash struck the ground off to her left. She threw her hands over her ears, but the thunder reverberated in her brain, loud and scary. Shaking her head to make her ears stop hurting, she set off again.

Lightning struck inches from her feet. Sam lurched to a stop and blinked to clear the afterimage. Even as wet as it was, the air felt electrified, thick with sharp edges. She could almost see marauding electrons reaching for her, hungry little bastards with their mouths wide open.

Fear raced along her nerve endings, making them jangle as if she'd downed half a dozen double espressos in a row. Breath whooshed out of her, and her head spun crazily.

The storm's trying to kill me.

Oh, please.

Sam hated her tendency to engage in two-way inner dialogue, but she'd done it all her life.

An excruciating twenty minutes and half a dozen lightning strikes later, she thought it might be safe to move. It continued to rain like a son of a bitch, but after striking a circle around her, the electrical part of the storm departed as precipitously as it arrived.

Guess the storm gods didn't want me, after all.

Why should they? No one else does, and now I'm dumped and drenched.

Sam giggled. Dumped and drenched held a kind of alliterative twang, but her next chortle skirted the edge of hysteria. Shit, could she possibly be any wetter? Weather in the British Isles had been particularly wretched this summer, at least according to the locals. She suspected it always sucked.

"Yeah, sort of like the rest of my life," she muttered as she tried to assess if she'd be better off staying on the track or cutting cross-country toward where she thought a roadway was.

Resolutely, she struck out for the road and promptly stepped into calf-deep water. It ran over the top of her boot and soaked her thick, woolen sock before she could jerk her foot back to solid ground.

So much for that idea. The drenching rain had turned the ground on both sides of the track into a bog. She'd never seen one before this trip to Scotland. They were hideous. Miles of saturated ground with water deep enough to reach her knees in some places.

Sam glanced at her watch and groaned. She'd been walking for close to five hours. No wonder it was getting dark. The village she was aiming for shouldn't be far away. In fact, she should've already been there. About to tuck her watch back under her sleeve, she took one last look at it and realized the second hand had stopped. She tapped the crystal but nothing happened.

Crap! Wonder when it quit? Must be the damp.

Yes, another less pleasant voice piped up. *It also means I have no idea how long I've been walking.*

Peering through mist-shrouded countryside, she looked for signs of Beauly Village, but all she saw were sheep.

Sam kept walking. It wasn't as if she could take a break and sit to consider her options. Everything dripped water. Her jacket and pants, which had always provided sufficient protection from the elements back in the States, were wretchedly inadequate here. She was afraid to pull out her cell phone. Electronics and water definitely weren't compatible. Just look what happened to her supposedly waterproof watch.

Dark thoughts crowded her mind, and her efforts to squelch them failed.

Why had she thought it would be romantic to spend a year in Scotland?

An inner voice—the nasty one—sneered a reply. *Clint. Pretty man at first, but more like a pretty con man after I scratched the surface.*

Sam awarded her resident maven a point for accuracy. Clint, with his spiffy Scottish intonations, dreamy blue eyes, and red-blond curls, had sweet-talked her into bankrolling a trip to his home. Between his ever-so-broad shoulders, washboard abs, and nice, tight ass, she was so infatuated they'd barely left her bed for a month. She was head over heels in lust. And hoping desperately this time it would lead her to the altar.

Eager to grant her prince whatever he wanted, she readily agreed when he talked longingly of going back to Scotland for a while—before they got married. He wanted her to meet his family and arrange things with his parish priest. Except he had a personality transplant practically the second they landed in Glasgow. In the month-and-a-half since they arrived, she'd scarcely seen him. He was always off with his *mates*, as he called them, drinking or climbing. There were weeks when he hadn't returned to their rental flat in Inverness at all.

No sign of his family. Certainly no parish priest. Though she didn't want to admit the truth, it snuck in anyway. He'd never had any intention of introducing her to anyone, let alone marrying her.

When she took a good hard look at his *mates*, she wondered if he might be gay and asked if he swung both ways. Rather than answering, he'd twisted away and slammed out of the house, his blue eyes like chips of ice.

She hadn't seen him since. Probably a good thing, but it didn't hurt any less.

Water ran off the bill of her hood. Some of it dripped into one eye. "Oh to hell with it," she snarled. "I'm catching the first plane out of here—without him." She cursed her stupidity, feeling sad and angry by turns. Clint wasn't the first man who'd taken advantage of her. As soon as they found out she was heiress to a whiskey fortune, they promised her the moon and then fleeced her for everything they could get.

She'd gotten pretty cagey in the years between sixteen and her current twenty-five, even renting a modest apartment in Seattle and pretending she lived there when she met someone new.

Eventually, though, when she thought a guy might be different, she took him to the Capitol Hill mansion she'd more-or-less inherited after her parents relocated to one of their many other homes. No matter how promising a relationship looked, the truth of that rambling mansion spelled the beginning of the end.

Her mother had talked her into coming to Zermatt the previous year, luring her with a promise the men were simply amazing. After five frustrating weeks, Sam booked a ticket on the first departing plane that had space and fled.

Granted, she only dated a handful of guys in those few weeks, but she'd met enough to discern that Swiss men were insufferably straight-laced. Until they got her alone. Then they were all over her. And not in a good way. Even after she sidestepped their advances, they still told her how much they looked forward to being a part of her rich family, and went home. No cuddles, no endearments, not so much as a *what nice tits you have, my dear...*

Sam blew out a frustrated breath. All it did was rearrange the water dripping down her face.

"Goddamn it," she muttered. "I hate this place. Those Scots are a hardy bunch of bastards. If they weren't, they'd all have committed suicide centuries ago."

Lights flickered ahead, and Sam forced herself to hurry. Beauly Village. Finally. She'd been considering digging through her small backpack for her iPhone—and holding herself back. As it was, it hadn't liked the damp climate at all and became increasingly cantankerous after she dropped it in a puddle the previous week.

Even if I got the phone out, who the hell would I call? Do they even have a 9-1-1 system here?

Sam felt foolish—and angry with herself. Being lost scarcely qualified as an emergency. She peered through the murk at the lights and kept going, except they didn't get any closer.

Lots of reasons for that.

It's the fog.

My sense of time is distorted because I've been out here so long.

No matter how many reasons she came up with, an uncomfortable sensation lodged in her throat and refused to leave...

To go right on reading, here's a link to the book's page on my website. https://www.anngimpel.com/?portfolio=shadows-in-time

Tumble into a world where magic won, but the price was high enough to annihilate almost everything—including love.

Life in a shifter bordello is all Keira has ever known. None of the magicians' guilds wanted her because of her mixed blood, and they didn't protest when the shifters bound her as an indentured hooker. Mired in hopelessness, she longs for more.

Barrett's a full-blood magic wielder who operates a magician supply shop in what's left of Seattle. No one is more surprised than him when the Sidhe leader commands him to extricate Keira from the shifters. She loves to while away time in his shop, but she always skitters away whenever he even thinks about approaching her. Too bad because she's twenty shades of gorgeous.

Magic and intrigue throw Keira and Barrett together. but she has other priorities—like learning to control brand new magic she had no idea she possessed. Besides, once he spirits her away from the shifters, his job is done. Far better to keep his distance and allow her to seize the destiny she was born for.

Now if only he could believe that...

Barrett bent over, hands on his knees. His limbs were heavy, weighted with weariness. Even the mud-streaked asphalt looked promising as a place to lie down, assuming he found some cover. He strengthened the magic surrounding him and sucked air. The goddamned humans and their atomic weapons had poisoned the atmosphere. It would hasten the end of the war, but at what price? He swept his gaze over an uninterrupted vista of gray. The sky, clouds, remaining buildings, and ground were all the same depressing color. He didn't have to try very hard to hear the Earth cry and curse her guardians, the Sidhe, for doing such a piss poor job protecting her.

"The Weres, Druids, and Witches are ready to talk. The Fairies agreed to mediate." A familiar voice sounded from behind him.

Barrett straightened and turned to face Caelin. With the Daoine Sidhe queen long dead, Caelin was their de facto leader. All the other Sidhe answered to the Daoine, so he was responsible for thousands of them. Too bad he hadn't thought of that before dragging them into the war.

"Nice of them to consent to parlay while there's still something left to salvage," Barett muttered.

"Isn't it, though?" Caelin's customary sarcasm rang through. He spread his arms wide. "That last atomic blast decided things."

Tall and wraith-thin, Caelin looked about as trashed as Barrett felt. His shoulders sagged. Bright red hair had escaped his warrior braids and hung to his waist in tangles. His battle leathers drooped in tattered shreds. Bits of grit, leaves, and dirt mingled with everything. His sharp-boned face was streaked with grime, and he regarded Barrett intently out of dark blue eyes.

"Maybe it's for the best." Barrett met Caelin's gaze. "We've been fighting for close to ten years. If the humans hadn't felt threatened and pulled out all the stops, this might have turned into a hundred-year war —if any of us lived that long."

Caelin snorted. "We coexisted with those bastards for thousands of years. The minute they got a whiff they weren't the only ones on the planet, they overreacted."

A corner of Barrett's mouth twisted wryly. "You have to admit magic can be a bit off-putting for humans."

"Well, they fucked themselves."

"That may be so," Barrett retorted," but we instigated their reaction. It might've been accidental, but our magic did kill them. They had no idea their deaths fell into the collateral damage category and pulled out bombs to retaliate."

Caelin shook his head. "Didn't work well for them, did it? There won't be very many left once the atomic dust settles."

Barrett quirked a brow at his leader. "To borrow from your vernacular, they've managed to fuck us too, by dying. We're going to have to figure out how to keep things running without them."

"Point taken. Be sure to toss it on the table when we draw up a Covenant with the other magic wielders." Caelin shook his head. "Despite all our efforts, there are more Weres left than any of the rest of us—"

"Only because they breed like rabbits."

Caelin waved him to silence. "Be that as it may, we must secure their cooperation. Otherwise, our numbers will be far too small to maintain any semblance of civilization. I'm talking about infrastructure, things like electricity, water, the Internet, the cellular system, and food." He ticked them off on his fingers as he talked. "All the things humans used to take responsibility for. It's fortunate enough structures are still standing to house most of those left."

"Where and when is this meeting scheduled?" Barrett hoped he could catch a few hours of sleep. He'd been up for the better part of the last two days.

"It's now. In the Opera House since it's mostly intact. Walk with me." Caelin set off at a moderate pace.

Barrett caught up to him. His muscles ached. A headache pounded behind one eye. Normally, he would've used magic to ease both, but he was seriously depleted. What little remained of his power was focused on filtering subatomic particles out of the air before it entered his lungs, so the radioactive fallout didn't damage him. "I still wish—"

"Don't say it. Even in my worn-out state I have enough magic left to read your thoughts." Caelin set his jaw in a stubborn line Barrett recognized only too well. The Daoine Sidhe leader had never liked being questioned, nor was he open to discussion about his decisions.

Fine. Read my thoughts then. You can pretend they don't exist, but we both know differently.

The loss of their queen, Ivanne, had heated the rift between the Weres and the Sidhe to a boiling point and proven disastrous. She'd been a skilled mediator, navigating difficult political waters with grace and skill. Caelin was a warrior. He saw the world in black and white. Convinced the Weres had murdered Ivanne, he'd convened the Council, dominated it with his anger, and led the Sidhe to war. At first it was just Sidhe against Weres. Then Witches and Druids jumped into the fray, some on one side, some on the other. The only magical beings who'd remained neutral were the Fae and the Fairies.

"The Weres poisoned Ivanne. Her death demanded retribution." The harsh gravel of Caelin's voice broke into Barrett's thoughts.

Barrett grabbed Caelin's upper arm and forced the other man to a standstill. "Stop justifying yourself. War never solved anything. Not in human history, or in ours, either." He swung an arm wide. "Look. Just look what a mess we've made. It will take decades for Earth to recover, if she ever does. Deep in my soul, she reprimands me over and over for our part in the destruction."

A sheepish look flitted across Caelin's face. He ran a hand down it, distorting his features. "Glad I'm not the only one she nags."

A brittle anger filled Barrett, setting his guts on fire.

"We deserve to be nagged. More than nagged, we deserve to be chastised—"

"It's not like I did this singlehandedly." Caelin sounded defensive. "The Weres could've capitulated anytime."

Barrett let go of Caelin's arm. He pounded a fist into his open palm. "Damn it! You know better. Weres never apologize. They're constitutionally incapable of admitting they were wrong about anything. It's their dual natures. The animal side takes over and—"

"Spare me." Caelin thumped his hands on Barrett's shoulders, digging his fingers in hard enough to make Barrett wince. "If I made a mistake avenging Ivanne, it's water long passed under the bridge. Think, man. That was ten years ago. We must play the ball where it is today. There's little enough of our royalty left. Here in the Americas, it's you and me. I must have you standing solidly beside me. The Weres will sniff it out soon enough if we're not aligned with one another."

Barrett blew out a breath. Annoyance scoured his nerves. He hated to admit it, but Caelin was right. If the war was finally edging toward détente, the next task would be crafting a Covenant with terms advantageous to all Sidhe, not just the Daoine. And making certain it enlisted everyone's aid healing the damage done to Earth.

He ducked from beneath Caelin's hands, squared

his shoulders, and swept straggling copper-colored hair out of his face. "You need have no fears on that front. You have always had my allegiance and support." Of a height with Caelin, Barrett locked gazes with him. "You're a brilliant tactician. And a fearless warrior. I only wish you had a bit more in the way of warmth and compassion to temper things."

A wry grin split Caelin's face. He didn't smile often. The effect was electrifying, bringing his latent beauty to the forefront. He punched Barrett lightly. "I wish for a lot of things too. Problem is I rarely get any of them." He inclined his head in a mock bow. "After you."

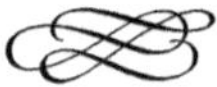

Eleven Years Later

Keira opened her door and peeked out into the long hallway spanning the first floor of Were Calls, the Were bordello where she lived and worked. Empty. *Good.* It was the middle of the afternoon, always a slow time. Her last customer had just left. Maybe, if she snuck out the rear door, she could claim a few hours of freedom. She ducked back into the room she shared with one of the other indentured hookers, donned a cloak and boots, and walked down the hall, making as little noise as possible.

The air was crisper than she'd expected as she eased the door shut behind her. Keira wrapped her arms around herself, wishing she'd brought a warmer coat. Most of her working clothes were wispy and suggestive. At least she'd been smart enough to put on tattered jeans, a moth-eaten sweater, and her favorite black cloak. For once it wasn't raining. A pallid sun hung midway to the western horizon, bathing what were once busy urban streets with sallow light.

Keira emptied her mind, trying not to feel like she was playing hooky. It wasn't as if the Weres kept her prisoner... She glanced at her left arm. Under the sweater and cape, she could've sworn the indenture bracelet spanning her upper arm tightened.

Who am I trying to kid? They can find me anytime they want.

She walked briskly through Seattle's Queen Anne district. Keira had the streets to herself today, but then she usually did. Good thing too. Those like her, mixed-blood magic wielders with minimal power, were at pretty much everyone else's mercy. Bottom of the New World totem pole.

She gazed over urban rot, some parts worse than others, and grimaced. Buildings still stood, a few of them, anyway. But most of the glass had been rocked out. Piles of trash blocked the roadways. Cars were a thing of the past. Out-of-control garbage had obliterated the sidewalks long ago. Paths wound through it, carved by varieties of magic wielders and prowling beasts. She made a point of ignoring what was underfoot. Most of it was too gross to even consider. It was a damned shame so many humans had been wiped out during the war. They'd taken care of things like garbage collection.

She pretended to consider what to do with her freedom, knowing her deliberations were a sham. She'd do the same thing she always did: head for Barrett's magician's shop. Housed in a cavernous Victorian on lower Capitol Hill, it was only about an hour's walk from the Were bordello. With its dark wood furniture, Oriental carpets, and overflowing shelves, the shop exuded an irresistible, homey atmosphere.

Face it. The thing that makes it so enticing is Barrett.

Keira smiled to herself as she pictured the tall, broad-shouldered Daoine Sidhe with his thick, coppery hair and pale blue eyes. Beyond his obvious beauty, though, he seemed kind. Not that she'd ever exchanged more than a few words with him, but he had laugh lines in the corners of his eyes, and she'd watched him interact with other customers. He was always helpful, doing that little bit extra to assist someone find something. There was still bad blood among magic wielders, but not in Barrett's shop. Everyone was granted equal status there. Never mind Daoine Sidhe magic was far more powerful than Were, Fae, or Witch. Druid magic barely counted; it was nearly as feeble as hers.

The first time she'd stumbled into Barrett's shop, it

was by accident. She'd gotten into a big blow up with Simon, one of the staff at Were Calls, for refusing to service a customer in his animal form. Simon slapped her, which was a big no-no. Punishment was supposed to be delivered through her bracelet per the terms of her indenture.

Keira had never seen Simon quite so angry, and she wasn't inclined to wait around to see what he'd do next. Despite being in her hooker garb, including high heels, she'd raced out the door and ran until her arches ached. It hadn't helped when the skies opened, and it began to pour. Not knowing what else to do—because she was *not* going back to Were Calls until things cooled down, or they zapped her through the bracelet—she opened her magic senses. They led her straight to Barrett's shop. It was only a couple of blocks from where she'd stopped.

Keira had pushed the heavy, carved wooden door open, ready to bolt if anyone so much as looked cross-eyed at her. No one did. The shop smelled heavenly. Herbs. Lots of them. They hung in bundles from a raised walkway, ten feet off the ground, which accessed a partial second story. Feeling a bit braver, she let her gaze roam about the large room, crowded with shelves. No one paid her the slightest attention, which was amazing since all the other patrons were garbed in cloaks and coats. She glanced at her low-cut top, barely-there micro mini, and high heeled boots and winced. Her top didn't leave much to the imagination since it was half-soaked through. Because she was cold, her nipples had pebbled into suggestive peaks.

Embarrassed, she skittered behind a bank of shelves and worked her way around the outside wall of the shop, appreciating being out of the weather. Her eyes widened at the variety of wares for sale. She lingered over things she couldn't identify and hustled past things she wanted but could never afford. Along the way, she summoned a tiny bit of magic to help dry her clothes.

Keira recalled hearing the Weres talk about Barrett's shop. It was the only place left that still sold magician's accoutrements and supplies. Three-quarters of the way through her transit of the shop, a musical baritone voice caught her attention. She stopped and looked for its owner. He stood behind the counter, wrapping a package and counting out change. Because he was occupied, it seemed safe to let her attention linger on him.

What a beautiful man. When he patted a Witch's hand before handing her the packet he'd wrapped, Keira wondered what those hands would feel like on her. The shop suddenly grew much warmer, and she bit back a laugh. Sex was plentiful in her life, no reason to moon over a man. Several would no doubt be waiting for her back at Were Calls.

She'd just decided to edge a bit closer to the counter, drawn by the Daoine Sidhe's magnetism, when the bracelet on her arm tightened. Keira ignored it, but it only tightened more. She knew how the game worked. The Weres tracked her with electronics. Once she headed for Were Calls, the bracelet would leave her alone—as long as she kept moving. If she stopped for too long once they'd warned her, the next event would be a shock.

Keira had scuttled out of Barrett's store that day, but she hadn't stayed gone long. Every time she left the bordello, it was where she ended up. She spun fantasies about what it would be like if she were free and could offer to work for Barrett. Just the thought of being close to him for long hours each day made her heart speed up.

Don't be foolish, she chided herself as she reached the now-familiar door and pushed her way into the magic shop. *He's Daoine Sidhe. He'd never be interested in a mixed blood like me.*

She walked to a locked case with crystals and gazed at them. A beautiful rose quartz one she'd lusted over was gone. *Damn!* She'd been working up her courage to ask if she could hold it in her hand to feel its energy.

Keira never bought anything; she didn't have the

money. She'd felt apologetic her first few visits, but now that she'd been there so many times, she felt confident Barrett wasn't going to throw her out.

"Can I help you find something?"

Keira froze. It was him. She'd know Barrett's voice anywhere. She heard it in her dreams, and sometimes she imagined one of her johns was him. In her imagination, he crooned to her in that wonderful voice and...

He tapped her shoulder. "Miss. May I help you?"

Keira spun to face him. Her face heated, and she knew she had spots of color high on both cheeks. "Uh, no. I'm just looking." Responding to something, maybe a small spell, maybe just an invitation in those wonderful ice-blue eyes, she stammered on, "The rose quartz crystal—"

"I sold it. Just yesterday. It was one of my favorites as well. If you're interested, I should be getting a new shipment soon, but the crystals are all unique. If there's one you like, just let me know, and I can ascertain if it pairs well with your energy."

"I, um, you see, I can't really afford anything like that. I just like to look."

"It's okay. I get lots of lookers here."

Barrett smiled at her. Gazed into her eyes and smiled right at her. Keira's heart stuttered. She opened her mouth and closed it again when words wouldn't come. Unable to help herself, she took a step toward him and stumbled.

He placed a hand under her elbow to steady her. "Got you."

An electric shock ran up her arm. Her breathing quickened.

You don't know the half of it. You've more than got me.

Heart thudding, throat dry, she smiled, managed to murmur, "Thank you," and scuttled toward the door before she did something stupid like throw herself at his feet and beg him to take her.

Here.

Now.

On the floor in front of everyone.

Barrett gazed after the fleeing girl. His cock pressed against the front of his worn breeches, as hard as it ever got. It throbbed hotly, urging him to go after her, run her down, drag her back to his bed, and... He shook his head. What had gotten into him? He was well beyond the age where he let his penis lead him around.

The girl was unbelievably beautiful. Her blonde hair was so long it reached her ass. She had an arresting face with high cheekbones, lush lips, and silver eyes.

He'd thought only his race had eyes that color, and they were rare even among the Daoine Sidhe. But the ache in his groin went beyond her beauty. There was something about her, a purity of spirit that called to him. When he'd tried to sense her magic to see just what she was, he ran up against a wall. Almost as if she were warded. It wasn't something she was doing on purpose, though. If it was, he'd have seen it in her mind. No, it was more like a magical barrier surrounded her.

He usually didn't pay any attention to the hordes of customers frequenting his shop. After all, it was the only one of its kind left. He expected it to be full to overflowing with patrons. He'd noticed the girl, though, the very first time she snuck in. Wet to the bone, her full breasts, tipped with wonderfully erect nipples, had been clearly visible through the thin fabric of her top. She'd taken to the outer wall and worked her way around the shop that day. Curious about her, he'd spun a mild compulsion spell to reel her in closer. He still didn't know what happened. She'd been moving toward him when something shifted, and she scampered out of his shop like the dogs of Hell were nipping at her heels.

Sort of like she did today.

He chuckled, not caring that a pair of Witches eyed him oddly. He'd spoken with the girl a few times, but today's conversation was by far and away the longest. Though he liked to see himself as immune to women, this one frequented his dreams. He often woke with his hand pumping his shaft as he fantasized about the girl with no name. In his favorite vision, she was astride him, firm breasts pressed against his chest and long, blonde hair tickling his naked flesh.

Determined to at least find out where she lived before her trail grew cold, he glanced about the store. Too many customers to get rid of. He strode to Baen, a Witch who'd fought on their side during the war. "Could you watch the register for me? Sorry, but it's a bit of an emergency. I won't be gone more than an hour or two."

She raised perfectly formed red brows in her ageless, porcelain-skinned face. "For you. Of course," she purred.

"Thanks." Barrett kicked himself. He'd forgotten Baen had been trying to worm her way into his bed for a couple of years. Then he stopped thinking and sprinted out the door. Barrett threw his magic senses wide open, searching. He blew out a relieved sigh. There she was. Her track would be easy to follow. He'd been afraid the same magic that cloaked what she was would hide her trail as well.

He warded himself, so his power wouldn't tip her off and followed her back to Were Calls.

Son of a bitch. She's a hooker.

From his vantage point behind some stacks of trash, Barrett felt incredulous. How did the Weres ever get someone that gorgeous to trick for them? What he knew fell into place. She had to be indentured. It was why he couldn't get close enough with magic to sense what she was. The Weres must have some sort of microelectronic harness on her. He'd heard about them from the Fairies, who generated most electronic devices these days.

An indefinable sadness tugged at him. He felt the heaviness in the pit of his stomach. Barrett waited until the door shut. He'd heard a man shouting at the girl from where he was, all the way across the street. It was a struggle not to go pound on the door, tell them he'd buy her bond, and be done with it. Even if she didn't want him, at least she'd be free.

Barrett took a deep breath and then one more. *Get back to the shop*, he instructed himself sharply. *The last thing I need is emotional entanglements.* So he wouldn't be tempted to change his mind, he pulled magic, visualized his shop, and left in a hurry.

At least the girl wasn't a mystery anymore. It explained why she'd been so tentative in his shop. He was surprised the Weres let their property roam about freely, but then he remembered the Covenant. Even the indentured had some rights. Weres had been the only ones who wanted indentured servants. The others had argued vehemently against them. Especially the Fairies. In the end, the other magic wielders had capitulated because the Weres were ready to walk out on fragile negotiations. And they weren't signing anything that didn't let them keep their pet servants.

Barrett stood in front of his shop for a few moments composing himself. Now that he knew more, he'd have a better chance of approaching the girl next time she came to his shop.

I thought I didn't need any emotional tangles, an inner voice mocked him.

Barrett ignored it. He nodded to himself, certain she'd show up again. Something about his shop drew her. Maybe it was an antidote to the life she led. He pushed open the door and went inside.

"There you are." Baen settled a hand familiarly on his arm.

"Yes." He forced himself to smile brightly. "Thank you so much. Here." He broke away from her grip. "Let me pay you."

"Not necessary. Maybe I could stay for a bit after you close—" She leered suggestively and licked full, red lips.

Barrett blew out a breath. "I'm flattered, but no. I do not want you in my bed."

Her eyes widened. "I-I'm not sure where you got that idea," she sputtered, color staining her face.

"Because I'm very good at reading body language. And minds. Thanks for watching the shop. Now, if it's all the same to you, I'd just as soon end this conversation."

Her lips drew back into a snarl. Magic spooled so hot it turned the air incandescent. Barrett steeled himself, sure she was going to launch herself at him and go for his eyes. Instead, she spun on her heel and strode toward the door, hips swinging as if to say, *see what you missed, buddy.*

Barrett blew out a tired breath and settled himself in his customary seat behind the counter. He hoped there wouldn't be any repercussions from the Witches because Baen was angry. From long habit, he scanned the shop, alert for any sign of trouble. Today everyone seemed to be getting along. He shut his eyes. The girl materialized in the darkness, her silver eyes aglow.

Tomorrow, he promised himself. *Tomorrow, I'll at least find out her name...*

To go right on reading, here's a link to the book's page on my website: https://www.anngimpel.com/?portfolio=hearts-flame